Miserations More Still

Miserations More Still

Mike Gutowski

Miserations More Still

Mike Gutowski

Including the greatest 100 days in human history.

Miserations More Still is a work of fiction and philosophy. Names, characters, places, and incidents are the products of the author's imagination or are used fictitiously unless otherwise noted. Any resemblance to actual events, locales, or persons, living or dead, is entirely coincidental unless otherwise noted.

Cover artwork created by W.A.G.

For permission requests, contact the publisher, at:

Email: dadx3g@msn.com

Facebook: @mike.gutowski.62

softcover ISBN: 979-8-9873433-4-0

eBook ISBN: 979-8-9873433-5-7

Printed in the United States of America

Philosophy, Dark Fantasy, Dystopian Fantasy

First Edition

Still more rambles through the brambles of everyday life while searching for and experiencing the meaning of existence in the 21st century, including U.S.A. President 47's initial one hundred days in office, politics in general, mock-humanitarian poetry, and other unusual tidbits.

M.E.G. - -

<u>On Truth's Reality</u> 10/03/2024 09:25 PM

Truth is flexible. Reality is not.

<u>On Woke Human Nature</u> 10/04/2024 10:52 PM

Human nature has become woke cursed. This battle for survival probably took a thousand years off the general intellect evolution scale.

<u>On Love Reality</u> 10/05/2024 02:51 AM

Romantic love is essentially a fiction harped upon by all manners of marketeers from parental units to sex shops. Each promotes romance as a grand dance. It is often an essential illusion for the evolution of a species. A passion play. Clothing ensembles are designed to stoke the mood. Handy instruments inspire desires to run wild in the grasslands. Grunts, groans, shouts random, screams blaring, then an eerie relaxed silence of sweat and sour aromas permeates mystically the scene clouding over short memories of flesh friction inspirations as a restful nirvana ensues.

<u>On Universal Themes</u> 10/05/24 02:06 PM

The universe will never reveal its most intimate secrets. It knows better. It is an extension of its own inhabitants. It knows they will try to bend and shape it to their liking. A very naughty thought.

<u>On Think Sparks</u> 10/05/2024 05:57 PM

Emotional output shows paying attention. The analysis baked into attention phase is evoked by sound, physical contact, or memory. Analysis starts at an ignition point of thoughts forced to stream.

Force in the human mind shows an on off button. The button serves as a tuning mechanism mentally attached to a prosecuted potential response. Perspective maturity affects output response.

On Puppet Politics 10/06/2024 01:56 AM

Politics has become a Marionette show of broken strings and promises.

On Government Censorships 10/06/2024 08:34 PM

U.S. citizens do not want the elites and government agencies controlling censorship. U.S. citizens have a constitutional right to instigate authority over politicians and their cadre of elitists and media propagandizers.

On Klimate Kookery 10/06/2024 09:21 PM

Climate worship seems to claim the insane.

On Hypocrite Hijinks 10/06/2024 09:34 PM

Every informal word battle entices a hypocrite versus hypocrite word war play.

Darkness Shine 10/06/2024 11:07 PM

Short Story Idea: "I am the night. I am the dark of light."

On Following Instructions 10/07/2024 01:00 PM

Just follow the instructions to find out why the result does not work.

On Temperamental 10/07/2024 01:12 PM

I have a temperamental light switch. Sometimes it works and sometimes it does not. Reading poetry ... helps me to cope with the issue.

On Broken Be's 10/07/2024 01:16 PM

Behoove and behave are mutually exclusive.

On Whispers of the Wind 10/07/2024 11:33 PM

To end a pandemic or other human scourge upon any society it is necessary to extinguish permanently the origin of the destruction force past, present, and future. In other words, turn the scourge into whispers of the wind.

On Futurist Mechanisms 10/07/2024 11:57 PM

It is easy to figure out the futures of most societies in every country. Brainwashing methods and the entities that use them: Teachers and institutions of learning; Big Tech moguls; Media mind mushers; Religious institutions; corruptocratic politicians. All molding the minds of the sheeple.

On A Love's Kiss 10/08/2024 04:04 AM

The greatest salvation imaginable when lovers embrace each other's company is the palliative exhilaration of an honest and palpable mutual kiss. Other sensations flee the mind in a heartbeat. It is a mind fuck.

On An Author's Thoughts 10/08/2024 04:10 AM

Chaos is the tentative inspiration inflicted upon any author's mind: ideas and facts crash together while tethered to a tangle of knots. Never know when the chaos part of even a planned session will take over and rule the story line of characters and scenes in which they find themselves placed to confront each other.

On Mind and Body Collaboration 10/08/2024 04:17 AM

There are two ignitions in the mind and body cohabitation process: an ignition of thought and then an agitation of physical action.

On Human Meetings 10/08/2024 04:20 AM

Every personal encounter involves a question chasing an answer.

On Energy at Rest Confusions 10/08/2024 04:27 AM

The mind develops a nature of wanting to know. From then on, questions and answers never stop an inquiry process. The impact can be seen and heard in noticeably young children. Similar to a car engine that does not start with a turn of the ignition key or a button press. Also similar to a tired human body unable to rest when the mind's thought ignitions refuse to shut down.

On Genius Jealousy 10/08/2024 09:43 PM

Sometimes geniuses can only be recognized by genius minds and such minds may then seethe with jealousy sublime.

On 21st Century Life 10/08/2014 10:15 PM

If we want our children to learn absolutely nothing about life and how to live safely and successfully, then let us just allow Big Tech, Big and Little media, the Education Departments of the country keep doing what they are doing: complete destruction of reality, facts, logic and a means to develop the human mind.

On Government Truths 10/08/2024 11:14 PM

An honest government doesn't create more problems than it fixes.

On Sentience 10/10/2024 01:09 AM

What's known isn't often accepted.

On Constitution Salience 10/10/2024 11:39 AM

The single most sentient and stringent concept of a constitutional republic is the moral principle that government serves their masters who are the citizens. When that principle is chipped and swept away out the door into a street gutter, then the government becomes poorly diverted sewage water.

On Destiny 10/11/2024 08:54 PM

Destiny is a choice, and too, it has a voice.

On Politicians Usual 10/14/2024 10:20 AM

Who thinks a money laundering politician would assure the vote count is accurate?

Book Title 10/14/2024 11:01 AM

"How A Government Kills Citizens: A Manual."

On Noble Governments Ruined 10/14/2024 11:04 AM

The U.S. government of 240 years ago, envisioned by the founders, is today unrecognizable. It has become a machine operated by untrustworthy politicians for an undesirable sole purpose, used to enslave the legal citizen. It is now only capable of oppression.

<u>On Death Merchants</u> 10/14/2024 11:18 AM

When considering a politician's worth, a category called "Deaths" must be considered. In the U.S., 20 million largely unvetted humans from around the world have been permitted entry into the country. A minimum of 2 million are completely unknown. It is the largest invasion of any country in the shortest time in all human history. The mayhem, destruction, and death statistics have been fudged by the government in charge to protect their combined nefarious interests from discovery. The citizens regularly inquire about themselves: What to do about it?

<u>On The Beginning</u> 10/14/2024 04:13 PM

If we can't adequately explain the origin of the universe then we can't adequately explain the origin of a god.

<u>On Pickles Joy</u> 10/14/2024 04:35PM Aroma mellow and relaxed. Bite and chew moments crisp and flexible. Exuded juices refresh like a servile balm.

<u>English Literature</u> on Facebook 10/14/2024 09:36 PM

"It was not the truth they wanted, but an illusion they could bear to live with." Anai Nin, French born American diarist, essayist, and author (1903-1977)

<u>The philosoph</u> on Facebook 10/14/2024 09:44 PM

"You are never too old to set another goal or to dream a new dream." C.S. Lewis

<u>On gods Plan</u> 10/15/2024 10:45 AM

If there exist gods, then they are certainly not benevolent. They gave us land with no instructions attached.

<u>As Above So Below</u> on Facebook 10/15/2024 01:23 PM

"Those who are able to see beyond the shadows and lies of their culture will never be understood, let alone believed, by the masses." Plato

<u>On Twain Isms</u> 10/16/2024 03:00 PM

"Censorship is telling a man he can't have a steak just because a baby can't chew it." Mark Twain

"If voting made a difference , they wouldn't let us do it." Mark Twain

<u>On Hypocrisy Hills</u> 10/16/2024 03:10 PM

If misinformation and disinformation is deemed dangerous, then why are Big Tech, politicians, and media outlets permitted to speak and spread it. If it is dangerous, then why are only the common citizens not permitted to spread it.

<u>Twitter / X Posted Conversations</u>

Brian Krassenstein @krassenstein·Oct 16

Where is Trump's MSNBC interview?

Mike Gutowski @dadx3gMike·23h 9:11 PM · Oct 16, 2024

there's no point to MSNBC, so there's no point to an MSNBC vivisection.

Walter Kirn @walterkirn·Oct 16

Don't understand why Dems oppose "disinformation" when they slosh out so much of it

Quote

Lev Parnas @levparnas·Oct 15

BREAKING: Sources close to the Trump campaign reveal a state of panic post-Pennsylvania Townhall. Insiders are scrambling, with whispers of Trump's mental capacity in question. Campaign insiders, once stalwart, now whisper worries if he can last the next 21 days.

Mike Gutowski @dadx3gMike·23h

On Miserations More Still 9:26 PM · Oct 16, 2024

"If misinformation and disinformation is dangerous, then why are Big Tech, politicians, and media outlets permitted to speak and spread it."

(from my next novella WIP, Miserations Still More)

Mike Gutowski 5:54 PM · Oct 17, 2024

@dadx3gMike·2h

Re: The Al Smith dinner.

@realDonaldTrump should ask @VP Harris the following questions: How old is the Earth? How old is the Universe?

Mike Gutowski @dadx3gMike

I did some research which might explain @VP Kamala Harris political beliefs. They seem to come from a perspective of Christian churches that embrace Creation Science. In other words, Earth is only 6,000 years old. Media needs to ask her the question. @IngrahamAngle @greggutfeld @seanhannity @elonmusk @BretBaier @maddow

Elon Musk @elonmusk·6h

This is illegal

Quote

Ian Miles Cheong @stillgray·13h

Around a hundred UK Labour politicians are campaigning on behalf of Kamala Harris across battleground states. Isn't this foreign election interference? Imagine if members of the Russian Duma did this.

Readers added context they thought people might want to know

The FEC explicitly permits foreign nationals to serve as campaign volunteers fec.gov/help-candidate...

Do you find this helpful?

Context is written by people who use X, and appears when rated helpful by others. Find out more.

Mike Gutowski @dadx3gMike·1h

On FEC Hypocrasy 6:56 PM · Oct 17, 2024

Well now that's a mighty curious circumstance. Where was the FEC when the Democrat controlled House of Representatives filed impeachment charges against President Trump? Was the FEC busy sucking Democrat party teats?

Elon Musk @elonmusk·1h

We need a video gamer voting block!

Make Games Great Again!!

Mike Gutowski @dadx3gMike·1h

On Video Gamer Voting Block 7:10 PM · Oct 17, 2024

I only play Risk and Chess online. not sure i'm qualified, but there are many exquisite and elite video games players worldwide. I come across some of them in the Recreation and Entertainment tagged categories. great idea.

Buck Sexton @BuckSexton·Oct 16

I've seen enough

Kamala is done

Trump is winning this election

Zero doubts

Mike Gutowski @dadx3gMike·1h

On Enough Seen 7:17 PM · Oct 17, 2024

i recently did some research on her religious beliefs based on how she avoids science questions. a possible conclusion is she believes the Earth and Universe have existed for only about 6,000 years. i posted about it an hour ago.

Freedom 7 @conservfam7·1h

The Harris campaign is reportedly renewing asking Trump for another debate!

Do you think Trump should?

I personally don't think he needs to debate her anymore!

Mike Gutowski @dadx3gMike·45m

On Campaign Strategy 7:39 PM · Oct 17, 2024

i agree, too. No need for a debate with a candidate who essentially refuses to answer questions directly.

Elon Musk @elonmusk·19h

Who sends out the commands to the NPC media puppets? I'd like to meet them.

They should really use a thesaurus, so that every media outlet doesn't use the EXACT SAME words every time.

DogeDesigner @cb_doge·19h

All these outlets are controlled by the same people, and have the same script. "Testy"

Mike Gutowski @dadx3gMike·41m

the truth: their talking points come directly from the Democrat Party, every day of the week. i thought everyone already knew about that circumstance.

Elon Musk @elonmusk·15h

Imagine 4 more years of this getting worse

Mike Gutowski @dadx3gMike·21m

On 4 More Years 7:43 PM · Oct 17, 2024

they won't stop unless they are forced to stop. they are a crime syndicate business entity just like the Democrat Party itself. i'm quite sure they've scouted out all of the locations that are easily accessible for a takeover.

Walter Kirn @walterkirn 6h

Mediocracy

A political system of compulsory mediocrity ruled and administered and managed by mediocrities

MAMA

Make America Mediocre Always!

On Mediocrocy (Make America Mediocre Always)

Mike Gutowski @dadx3gMike·15m 7:44 PM · Oct 17, 2024

that's a catchy name, but there is a much older and well-known name: Democrat Party (aka Democratic Party, aka slang Slavery Party).

Elon Musk @elonmusk·2h

Politics is absurdly tribal!

Also, didn't realize Maddow was a billionaire

Mike Gutowski @dadx3gMike·18m

On Tribal Politics 7:56 PM · Oct 17, 2024

Misery and mayhem enrich the media owners. They literally help stoke it for profit, assisted by the FBI and many other State and Federal agencies. They will never accept a day when they are not necessary. They work to keep the mayhem train rolling.

On Aging Perspective 10/18/2024 07:46 AM

Kindness is a survival method and not a way of life.

On Journalism Principles 10/18/2024 09:18 AM

Judge a book by the cover? Judge a journalist by copy production? Judge a politician by their friends? Competence and fairness don't fit into such word combinations.

On Truth Charades 10/18/2024 09:23 AM

People hate truth like they hate poison ivy.

On Virus Rights 10/18/2024 09:26 AM

Abort the virus, and too, the creator of it.

On Voter Choice Ramifications 10/18/2024 09:57 AM

If a citizen still votes for the same political party that has abused them and their ancestors for 197 years, then they get what they deserve.

On Something Not Political 10/18/2024 10:23 PM

On the cusp of a weekend's eve may the happiness of potential rest leave a breath of fresh air ease.

On Nonsense Parades 10/19/2024 03:20 PM

When too much energy is exerted on nonsense, then nonsense rules the day to the detriment of sensical matters.

On Chaos Crushers 10/19/2024 04:47 PM

A balanced lifestyle naturally becomes a barrier against chaos mongers.

On Vegetarians 10/20/2024 01:24 AM

They like to eat fruit and vegetables, and they are quite adept using knives.

Rooster 10/20/2024 07:59 PM

Short Story

Old mama came out to axe the roosters neck. Rooster had a very busy and prosperous mating session in the morning, and still feeling frisky, killed old mama.

Free bird. Rooster now ruled the farm. But he couldn't stop there. He kept on trapping families into trying to kill him.

Old man came back from tending the fields and found old mama dead, blood streaming from her neck, skin shredded claw marks streamed blood down her face.

Old man knew the marks meant the rooster had revolted. A tractor from down the road pulled up onto his lands. It was a neighbor giving him the warning of the rooster's actions. "This revolution must be stopped. Stopped now."

On City Life 10/21/2024 11:57 AM

Drug dealers and gang bangers feel safer than citizens do. Where? Most generally in Democrat Party run cities and environs.

On Life Fittings 10/21/2024 01:24 PM

What fits and what doesn't fit adequately serves the very being of every creature's life experience.

On Politics Rust 10/21/2024 05:30 PM

The bottom has dropped out of our rusty bucket democracy thanks to corrupt politicians and those who wield the socialist shovel.

<u>On Effort</u> 10/21/2024 05:43 PM

Where there's a will there's a way, just as where there's ill will, there's a broken path.

<u>On Pharmacy Renown</u> 10/22/2024 12:19 AM

"The CVS and the Odyssey" will an eon hence become renowned as an ancient mysterious Big Tech "Pharmaceutical Age" classic.

<u>On What Is Never Mended</u> 10/22/2024 09:36 PM

How can you mend a broken heart? Impossible to do so completely. It becomes a scar that never completely heals. One of the infamous drawbacks of emotional reality.

<u>On Journalism / Media</u> 10/22/2024 10:53 PM

Journalism and Media has been designated by some half-wit long ago as the Fourth Estate. This Estate has serially and physically injected itself into any subject matter but has evolved into a Fifth estate of filthy lie generation spraying regularly such lies upon the populace at large. A synonym for each entity is propaganda and propagandists. Each is married at the hip. Each resides in the communication junkyards regularly visited by corrupt politicians and hired proxies.

<u>On Life Moment Memories</u> 10/23/2024 03:24 AM

What are these days we waited so long for, longed for, never knowing what life mysteries laid in store. All asked was a chance at life not lonely, not filled with want and strife. Many times, happy days beamed bright. Many nights, we laid down wishing for one more morning light. Perhaps, these moments happened behind closed blinds somewhat frozen by harsh times. We pestered for the emotional serving bill at the "Memory Café" at one more lifetime thrill. One more lifetime thrill. One more lifetime thrill. One more lifetime thrill.

<u>End Times Concept</u> 10/24/2024 01:59 AM

End Time is a fictional concept that helps the human mind to close the front door and lock it. The concept seals the gap between the known and unknown portions of this world and the universe itself. In other words, a security blanket. Blankets can create comfort, but they are not intended for use as shields. Unknown is invisible to the mind. Known is an imperfect means of blending into the scenery.

<u>On Power Pukes</u> 10/24/2024 01:20 PM

The government is supposed to be our servant and not our master.

<u>On Stressors</u> 10/25/2024 05:34 PM

A sense of worry heightens stress levels but tends to increase concentration intensity.

<u>On Relevance</u> 10/26/2024 03:56 AM

What makes a moment relevant depends on contiguous circumstances devoid of sensibility except to the activated senses of a sentient mind.

<u>On Wedding Days</u> 10/27/2024 12:15 PM

Such joy metered by such stress annoyance. Still, the most beautiful day for all humanity given the future implications of the bond.

<u>On Political Magic Dark</u> 10/30/2024 02:30 PM

Politicians demand that citizens need them, and properly, such a demand enforced beams out as pure evil. See Europe and a Democrat Party run government as examples.

<u>On Chaos Talkin'</u> 10/30/2024 03:34 PM

Talkin' loud long is talkin' too loud long.

<u>On Rabid Foxes</u> 10/30/2024 03:58 PM

The political party that refuses Voter ID is a corrupt political party. Easier to trust a rabid fox than any politician.

On Malevolent Creatures 10/31/2024 10:53 PM No creature exists as malevolent as a politician.

On Death Shudders 11/01/2024 08:44 PM

Death hovers around us every day waiting for the perfect moment to assert itself. Decrease the odds it will succeed.

On Spaces 11/02/2024 03:03 PM

A nice room is a place where blame seeks no inhabitance.

On Peanut the Squirrel 11/02/2024 11:34 PM

Peanut the Squirrel's fate could be the Election story of this century. Essentially, quantifying exactly what a weird-world humans have created. Weirdgasmic.

On Past Possibility 11/04/2024 03:48 PM

What can be done about what has already been done? On what could have been poses a tempting answer.

On Political Genius 11/04/2024 04:12 PM

President Trump campaigned in long-standing deep blue and purple Districts as means to provide an opportunity to judge him face to face. Think about that strategy for a moment. Risked his life to do so.

On Voting Day 11/05/2024 02:03 PM

Many citizens voted to save the Republic.

On USA Pres Election 11/06/2024 02:43 PM

Revenge is never enough, or as now President 47 would say, "Sometimes by losing a battle you find a new way to win the war."

On Politics Tocks 11/06/2024 08:11 PM

Democrat power beats us down. Republican power raises us up.

On Life Weary 11/07/2024 02:54 PM

The world is a big place subject to ups and downs while traveling the little paths of life.

Out of Order

12/29/2021 03:39 AM

A cat's life, it is. He thought, Biz is.

01/20/2022 04:15 AM There aren't as many mysteries in living life as we might fool ourselves into thinking.

01/20/2022 04:17 AM

Sometimes we believe in something because it is true, and sometimes we believe in something because we want to believe in something.

01/20/2022 04:21 AM

What is difficult can be understood. What is easy can never be understood.

Back in Order

<u>On Tough Tasks</u> 11/11/2024 02:30 PM

The toughest physical tasks require an existential reckoning between body, mind, soul, and spirit.

<u>On Continued Learning</u> 11/11/2024 02:36 PM

Sometimes it's better to temporarily forget what one thinks they know in order to learn anew.

<u>On Blue State Governors</u> 11/11/2024 02:45 PM

Blue State Governors warn us about their power which is exactly why the sentient U.S. citizen rejects their corruption. When the Blue State citizens catch on, then they will become better off whether those Govs like it or not. The facts of these potential results are bubbling hot.

<u>On Life Investigations</u> 11/12/2024 05:23 AM

How a leaf falls. When a woman dances. Why a man struts. What a creature eats. Where a moment begins. Who cares.

<u>On Weather Anomalies</u> 11/12/2024 05:31 AM

The weather doesn't care. It must be accommodated and tolerated by all living things. It is cursed at or blessed depending on a moment's circumstance and convenience.

On Circumstance Conditions 11/12/2024 05:36 AM

When such and such and so and so first meet, a beautiful conundrum musically bloats and bleats.

On Science Philosophy 11/12/2024 05:39 AM

Make time to take time, or do the reverse. It's all fungible.

On Physical Perspectives 11/12/2024 05:50 AM

Something is moving in my mind from a far distance. I can't discern whether it is approaching or running away. It appears to be a human based on the limbs.

On Politics Evolution 11/15/2024 05:06 AM

The manner in which media blatantly promotes lies and varied political party election candidates simply displays large segments of the human population that have evolved less steadily than some other parts of the population.

On Universe Purpose 11/15/2024 05:15 AM

There must be a factual purpose to a universe existence, but no scientist yet has publicized such a reason. Caveat: faith is a creative fact process which essentially makes it part speculation and part fiction.

On Why 11/15/2024 01:53 PM

The most difficult question about existence is "why".

On Sympathy for the Devil 11/15/2024 06:02 PM

Democrats only want one thing: all of everything.

On Philosophic Thoughts 11/16/2024 07:08 PM

First comes interest, then attention, but prior to these mind states exists a trigger spark affecting the sentient mind. The trigger spark may happen at any time whether one is awake or asleep, experienced in any one of the known human senses. Science may refer to this action as atomical.

On Life Travails 11/18/2024 03:08 AM

Too many times, an idiot. Too many times.

On Choices 11/18/2024 03:10 AM

Wrong choices are best remembered to avoid a repetition unwise.

On Rules Unruly 11/18/2024 03:35 AM

When the rules of convenience outnumber the rules of survival then the culture rides upon a doom carousel.

On False Honesty 11/18/2024 04:20 PM

When accountability is absent then honesty becomes an afterthought, becomes a corruption of basic morals.

On Think Tinkering 11/19/2024 02:49 PM

A rearrangement of thoughts helps to lubricate the brain cells.

On Literature 11/20/2024 12:41 PM

What's the difference between a comic book and a Bible? Not a damned thing.

On Monetary Slavery 11/21/2024 01:25 PM

If money is the root of all evil, then why do we regularly send it to governments? We are paying for our own enslavement. The government is a slave master.

On Action Plans 11/21/2024 11:51 PM

The best way to pursue any task is with a planned purpose during a rigorous and curious mindset. Adjustments in the purpose, plan, and destination may be required as needed. If the dots don't connect then there's a hole in the final analysis.

On Governance Sublime 11/23/2024 02:36 PM

A responsible government gives more honestly than it takes corruptly.

On Reality Logic 11/23/2024 03:07 PM

Logic can become a crooked bastard that sucks its own dick.

<u>On Spaces Viscous</u> 11/24/2024 01:24 AM

The universe is a mindless spec of grotesquery. I see its face. The face transforms randomly, offering zero regards and even less rewards almost like a necessary evil. Boundless plenty at the cost of every life.

<u>On Socializing</u> 11/24/2024 08:51 AM

I really don't remember a time when I was unhappy being with you. Okay, finances. Okay, grouchy times. Okay, times I was ignored. But other than those moments … .

<u>On Common Sense</u> 11/24/2024 03:22 PM

We have reached the existence stage of humans claiming common sense is nonsense. A more than sad epoch of fime (Middle English word that means excrement, dung, or mud.)

<u>On Reality-Ish Takes</u> 11/24/2024 03:27

A-ish plus B-ish equals C-ish, and the X-ish plus Y-ish axis illustrates Z-ish.

Caveat: in government and politics each equation almost never adds up or illustrates a rational trend because necessary data is eliminated, or in fits sometimes does add up but reasoning of results remains a secret.

Presto: the reason why government budgets and science theorems are too often specious at best.

<u>On Poorly Learned</u> 11/24/2024 04:29 PM

Dumbasses kick themselves in the ass regularly. I suppose it could be considered a healthy exercise routine.

<u>On Quantum Computing Woes</u> 11/25/2024 02:37 PM

One day quantum computers will be able to predict the future, based on math calculations, for every human on the planet. Of course, the computers will be hacked, and the data will become corrupted.

<u>On Political Purges</u> 11/25/2024 05:38 PM

The 2024 U.S Presidential results portend a proper purge of corrupt political classes worldwide in scope.

<u>On Efforts' Travails</u> 11/25/2024 11:56 PM

It is not so much in the successes that we find ourselves. It is in the failures when the need for change and re-thinking arise to seize the hour, re-evaluate it, and then forge a better path to achievement. These are the moments of found glory for which the journey reaps rewards. A final success is a time to celebrate at the destination of a pleasant rest.

<u>On Learned Skills</u> 11/28/2024 12:36 PM

Intelligence is not wisdom. It is the seed of an apple requiring a nurturing environment. Take care of it. Allow it to grow responsibly. It will eventually rot if destiny time passes uneaten.

<u>On Indiscretion Thoughts</u> 11/28/2024 10:57 PM

If a person has a true heart, then any acts of indiscretion against another person will hound the mind. It is the brain reminding you to never stop loving. Proper caring leads to proper loving.

<u>On Speed of Freak</u> 11/28/2025 11:44 PM

The "anytime" speed.

<u>On Economic Policy</u> 11/29/2024 01:10 PM

Save the economy. Jail a corrupt politician.

<u>Shadows Within My Mind</u> on Facebook 11/29/2024 01:50 PM

"I want to write a novel about science. The things people don't say." Virginia Woolf

"Study without desire spoils the memory, and it retains nothing that it takes in." Leonardo da Vinci

<u>On Political Crimes</u> 11/29/2024 03:16 PM

If all of the crimes committed by the 46th President's administration were prosecuted, it would take a decade or more to resolve them all. Add the crimes of Congress and add another decade to the process.

<u>On Illusive Moments</u> 11/30/2024 04:07 AM

The more the night came, the more it went. These dreams of doom and dread. The more dread, the more the dreams, of times illusions bent. No more nightmares, he scolded the head. The mind nodded "No", but the heart still raised the curtain's show.

<u>On Time Trickles</u> 11/30/2024 04:16 AM

A moment lost is a moment stolen. A moment lost is a moment enslaved. A moment lost is a moment imprisoned. A moment lost is a moment forgotten. A feral cat, a stray dog, a cheatment of time. A phrase banished. A fast botch. A tickless clock. A wind rogue. A wasted vogue. A nonsense thought. An insult wrought. A lost brook. A checkmate rook. A simple fault. An empty vault. A crowd dispersed. A theater show rehearsed. A holey May. A whole missing part. An empty forest. A never used spice. A roll of the dice. Valor's prize depending on the eyes. A photograph torn. A child unborn. A package undelivered. An invitation unsent. An effort unspent. A thought banished. A dream famished. A word tarnished. A space keenly varnished. A book unopened. A movie clip lost. A theory shattered. A fact splattered. A house torn down. A home unwound. A fog's haze. A nameless daze. A song too often heard. A silent bird. A silence not long enough scored. The account bored. A friendship faded. A skill set graded. Memories turn into dust as sometimes they must. Rust degrades mettle in the way lust degrades love.

<u>On Species Thoughts</u> 11/30/2024 03: PM

Humans are not what they're cracked up to be. None of them are. Not even me.

<u>On Life</u> 11/30/2024 03:36 PM

Dings and dongs. Bings and bongs. That is life.

<u>On Truth Secrets</u> 12/01/2024 03:24 AM

If truth is a legitimate construct, then there is no need to hide it like a broken doll.

<u>On Teaching Propers</u> 12/01/2024 03:30 AM

Teaching is helping others to learn necessary life skills. It is not instructing on what propaganda must be learned other than examples and purpose. It is not instructing on what teachers "want" learned. The teaching institutions have been grossly tainted by politics and person opinion perspective. If parents and children want that they can read the newspapers.

<u>On the Political Fates</u> 12/01/2024 09:00 PM

The moral of this story is to believe a corrupt politician is to seal one's own fate in misery.

<u>On Fun Paradox</u> 12/01/2024 11:24 PM

Having fun isn't a drug unless you let it become one. To overdose is to lessen the purpose.

<u>On Governed Corruption</u> 12/02/2024 01:31 PM Corrupt governments don't prosecute criminals if they benefit the government's mission to keep all non-preferred citizens enslaved.

<u>On Socializing Medication</u> 12/03/2024 11:30 PM

Wouldn't it be nice to live in a world where you can buy a personality to fit neatly into the social group you engage with during any particular get-together?

<u>On Book Writing</u> 12/04/2024 02:40 AM

Give the reader a good reason in every typed word to continue reading onward a sentence, paragraph, and chapter.

<u>On Love Lorn</u> 12/06/2024 03:00 PM

Love is a derivative of friendship, and many friendships are a scam born of need and driven by that need. Still, many are not joined by such an abrasive bond. These many are bonded by truth however slippery the ride.

<u>On Humanity Tidbits</u> 12/06/2024 04:53 PM

Remember, as humans we are the imperfect judging the imperfect.

<u>Shadows Within My Mind</u> on Facebook 12/06/2024 05:04 PM

"The advantage of a bad memory is that one enjoys several times the same good things for the first time." Friedrich Nietzsche

<u>EarthSky News</u> 12/07/2024

Fomalhaut, sometimes called the Loneliest Star in the southern sky.

<u>On Time Mending</u> 12/08/2024 03:07 AM

No adhesive exists to mend a broken promise. What cannot be mended can never be completely healed.

<u>On Orgasmic Possibilities</u> 12/08/2024 04:00 AM

Essentially, only 2 types of orgasms exist in the human body politic: orgasm sexual and orgasm intellectual. Each tracks a similar sensation path.

<u>On Gender Relevance</u> 12/08/2024 04:10 AM

From the perspective of the living dead, gender becomes irrelevant. Biological decay comes to life. Chemistry plays like a high school prom band named after the lonely sky star Fomalhaut.

<u>On the Human Condition</u> 12/08/2024 04:21 AM

It is impossible for humans to completely conceive

of the world in or on which they exist. After roughly 300,000 years of observation and study, much of the knowledge gained has already been lost during unnatural causes like war, and natural causes like diseases and famines. Further, the misuse of nature's gifts by humans has resulted in many means to cause premature death by invented methods of mass destruction such as development of viruses, gases, atomic and sub-atomic reactions, and pharmaceutical developments. We may consider ourselves the dominant species in our solar system, but the universe may beg to differ in perspective.

<u>On Citizen Worth Perspective</u> 12/08/2024 04:42 AM

Our politicians consider us their grapes pickers.

<u>On Unvisited Places</u> 12/08/2024 05:20 AM

I know as much about the after-life as I do about Paris, and I've never been to either.

On Writing Quandaries 12/09/2024 03:50 AM

If it can't be figured out, then figure it in.

On Chores and Jobs 12/09/2024 03:51 AM

When there's more to do then there's less to do when done.

On Luck's Charms 12/09/2024 03:53 AM

A fair wind gifts good results.

On Loud Small Sounds 12/09/2024 03:57 AM

A sudden whisper echoes loudly through the mind.

On a Human Quasar 12/09/2024 04:05 AM

The sight, sound, and aroma of a woman ignites the quasars in a human mind. Perhaps what the gods intended.

On Life Simplicities 12/10/2024 08:23 PM

A simple truth can be consider ruthless.

On Media Truth Ability 12/10/2024 08:26 PM

It's a 21st century given that media is chock full of idiots sublime. Rare exceptions exist.

A Company of Souls 12/11/2024 04:00 AM

Only a full seeks the company of idiots.

On Bodily Expenditures 12/11/2024 04:42 AM

Cost of action is use rate of energy, mind, and time.

On Democrat Economics 12/11/2024 12:06 PM

If I had a choice between Janet Yellen and a cornfield scarecrow to advise the country on economics, then I would choose the scarecrow.

On World Leaders 12/12/2024 03:23 PM

Canada and the USA currently display similar leaders: knick-knacks Trudeau and Biden sittin' on a bookshelf.

On Salt in the Wounds 12/12/2024 03:29 PM

Time is a bitch and bastard twist dance. At some point in our lives, we are all new, used and recycled.

<u>On Parody</u> 12/12/2024 04:24 PM

21st century vapid rapid.

<u>On Taxation Successive Excessive</u> 12/12/2024 05:33 PM

Corruption is saying you've never been taxed enough. The U.S. citizen of advanced age has lived under Federal, State, Local, Business, Fee, Usage, Property and multiple other types of "existence" taxes their whole lives. They're even taxed for dying. Essentially, living in slavery, monetized by governments. Upon retirement from the grind, citizens would appreciate a bit of a break from the immoral, enforced, swung, flung and flying government corruption hammer.

<u>Shadows Within My Mind</u> on Facebook 12/12/2024 07:25 PM

"If you're lonely when your alone, you're in bad company." Jean-Paul Sartre

<u>On Human Evolution Histories</u> 12/12/2024 09:31 PM

What if humans were the dominant species on another planet in our extant solar system billions of years ago but botched the effort to maintain such a status and thus became a lesser dominant species taken over by another humanoid species on the same planet?

The entire solar system is estimated to be about 4.5 billion years old, and Jupiter is 100 million years older than the other identified planets. If climate conditions changed naturally or unnaturally (due to human failure to adapt and attempt correction of a less hospitable environmental development) then a search for another atmosphere compatibility would have necessarily ensued. Strategically, another solar system world, such as Mars or Earth, may have been deemed survivable if a few DNA tweaks were instituted in a laboratory, then ejected into space directed towards the planets and / or moons intended to intersect those sun controlled orbital paths, hoping for success and adaptation / evolution of life forms on those physical locations.

Millions of years later, after penetration of Mars or Earth atmosphere and massive amounts of DNA plunked into each planets liquid and land incubator systems, what earthlings call "humans" may be better classified as "humanoid" offspring of Jupiter.

Using fantastical science fiction theories, the religious historical figures we call Jesus and comparable similar figures in other world religions may be representations of such humanoid inhabitants' origins. Is religion fantasy or fact based? Some civilizations believed they were formed by gods.

See Zoroastrianism, Egyptian, Roman, Greek, Islam, Hindu, Judaism, Confucianism, Taoism, Christianity, Roman Catholicism, Indigenous African religions, and many other cultures' spiritual beliefs as examples of human origin stories developed as means to seek connection points from Earth's existence point and off into other-worldly outer space or dimensional space prospective connections.

<u>On A demi-god's Bad Day</u> 12/13/2024 12:39 AM

At dawn, a drunken hangover-plagued prison guard god, tripped out of bed and broke the gates housing hell's inhabitants.

7 million years later … .

<u>On Employer Hiring</u> 12/13/2024 02:13 PM

You hire a jackass, you get a jackasses work product and production quality. Coasters and Toasters and Nepotistic Narcissists.

<u>On Ghosts and Goals</u> 12/13/2024 02:30 PM

During the execution of any well-planned endeavor, never doubt whether a projected positive conclusion is possible. Adjustments in plans and purpose may arise, sometimes regularly, but don't let these necessary changes cloud the means and measures required to reach the anticipated useful goals.

<u>On Political Principles</u> 12/13/2024 04:45 PM

Don't give anyone power to lessen your power.

<u>On Simple Tenets</u> 12/13/2024 04:49 PM

47 is the President-Elect because of his intent: to further empower the U.S. citizen.

<u>On World Peace</u> 12/13/2024 05:09 PM

An orgy of world peace awaits at the doorstep if only world leaders would venture upon the first step piece.

<u>Shadows Within My Mind</u> on Facebook 12/15/2024 12:37 PM

"An intellectual says a simple thing in a hard way. An artist says a hard thing in a simple way." Charles Bukowski

<u>On Afterlife Entities</u> 12/16/2024 02:11 AM

He didn't mind occasional visits from the dead although their flesh aromas bore scents of wet soil tinged by sewage waters, but the ghost aromas bore scents in no parts fleshy. More like wet clothes, mothballs, and sometimes sweetened of flowery perfumes. After the COVID pandemics such aromas and scents became less intrusive nasally.

<u>On Love's Anomaly</u> 12/16/2024 02:27 PM

Love is less than a many-splendored thing and is more than a fractured fairy tale.

<u>On Government Greed</u> 12/17/2024 04:23 PM

When the government comes around and says "we're taking everything you've earned and own because you don't deserve it", then it's time to disown that government.

<u>On This Universe</u> 12/18/2024 09:56 AM

This universe doesn't care when you were born, to whom, under what circumstances. Your fate is irrelevant in the great scheme of life. Such a harsh reality must not be mourned. Perhaps it acts like a curse to be more than sentient than other creatures who never seem concerned about such fates except for immediate needs.

Find purpose not in or for this universe. Find purpose for your inner being. This being is yours. Learn as much as possible about it to find relevance for your existence.

<u>On Politics</u> 12/18/2024 11:06 AM

The politicians want democracy for themselves but want socialism for everyone else.

<u>On Choices Suspect</u> 12/18/2024 07:46 PM

It is with significant willpower exertion that we should employ an effort to avoid becoming someone else's unwary fool.

<u>On New Words Creation</u> 12/19/2024 01:00 AM

Affalogic: noun, meaning angels forever, forever angels (affa) exhibiting the principles of reason.

Synonyms: alfalogic, betalogic, omegalogic, zetalogic.

<u>On Troublesome Thoughts</u> 12/20/2024 03:16 AM

When all hope seems lost, if the correct path remains followed then the traveler is not lost.

<u>On Life's Mysteries</u> 12/20/2024 03:28 AM

Troubling decisions in a person's life involve what

mysteries need to be resolved and in what proper order they need to be arranged.

<u>On Politics Transparency</u> 12/20/2024 02:29 PM

Honest politicians ring out as an oxymoron.

<u>On gods and Ego</u> 12/21/2024 01:29 AM

If someone thinks they are a god, then they are not a god, but merely a human of power who is possessed of a fool's ego.

<u>On Dream Travels</u> 12/21/2024 03:04 AM

Dreams are wished searching for a reality conclusion.

<u>A Second Beyond a Lost Breath</u> 12/21/2024 03:38 AM

Serenity is neither lightness nor darkness. It is nothingness. Absence of physical pains; a serene emptiness of further tasks or commitments. A return elementally to universe mysteries as yet to be discovered. A trip in the form of stardust. A relocation of the human senses to a place where those senses and emotions are no longer needed except for maybe re-energizing the stars. No form. No substance yet determined relevant or necessary except to those still living who have been and will be influenced by that sentience which has passed to them and into the beyond.

On Music for a Funeral 12/21/2024 02:24 PM

Layla, Derek and the Dominos; Money, Pink Floyd; Stairway to Heaven, Led Zeppelin; Funeral March, Chopin; The Moldau, Smetana; Better Man, Pearl Jam; Where the Streets Have No Name, U2; The Sound of Silence, Simon and Garfunkel; In The Dark, Billy Squier; Day After Day, Badfinger; Dream Weaver, Gary Wright; Nights in White Satin, The Moody Blues; All I Know, Art Garfunkel; In-A-Gadda-Da-Vida, Iron Butterfly; Summer Presto, Vivaldi; Whisper of Angels, Amici; Canon in D Major, Pachelbel; Alone, Heart; One in a Million, Larry Graham; A Whiter Shade of Pale, Procol Harum; Same Old Lang Syne, Dan Fogelberg; Do You Feel Like We Do, Peter Frampton; November Rain, Guns N' Roses; Purple Rain, Prince; Bringin' On the Heartbreak, Def Leppard; Night Games, Stephanie Mills; Un-break My Heart, Toni Braxton.

On Destination Planning 12/21/2024 02:55 PM

A struggle in life involves going to where one wants to go but not arriving at the time desired.

On Wedding Starts 12/21/2024 03:09 PM

When full of the madness of joy and emotion, after the experience, anything can happen.

On Human Intentions 12/23/2024 12:36 PM

Socializing is too many times a necessary evil.

On Politics Possession 12/23/2024 12:40 PM

Democrats are so insane. Their bigotry kicks up several notches once they find out someone isn't one of them.

<u>On Morning Joys</u> 12/23/2024 12:49 PM

Freshly brewed coffee is life's little blessing.

<u>On the Memory Engine</u> 12/23/2024 04:30 PM

He missed good times of the past. They were an engine of sharing current and future memories.

<u>On Seeing is Believing</u> 12/23/2024 06:58 PM

We can't even see ourselves in real time. A mirror

perhaps assists. We are expected to see others in real time. The paradox of existence is truly a rabbit hole.

<u>On Change</u> 12/23/2024 07:31 PM

Find yourself. If you don't like what you've found, then make some changes.

<u>On Selling "It"</u> 12/23/2024 10:36 PM

Everyone, at one time or another, becomes a car salesperson in demeanor, depending on the survival needs.

<u>On Religion Drive-Ins</u> 12/24/2024 09:30 AM

Would you like wine and bread sauce with that meal?

<u>On Sentience Pitfalls</u> 12/24/2024 04:24 PM

To know more is to realize less.

<u>On the Gift of Life</u> 12/24/2024 05:17 PM

Life is the gift that just keeps on tacking back what was given, by any means necessary. Yet, we can't speak with the giver face to face. We can only communicate with the giver's surrogates who talk in rhymes and psalms or read book passages to us. A somewhat diabolical circumstance given all the curtains that must be drawn to find what's in the box.

<u>On Solitude</u> 12/25/2024 09:23 PM

Lilly lies as sunset dies during ancient cries.

<u>On Calloused Words</u> 12/25/2024 09:29 PM

To speak ill is to infect will.

<u>One Sense Bites</u> 12/25/2024 09:29 PM

Let bygones flee the mind like tastes of lemons.

<u>On A Moments Propriety</u> 12/25/2024 09:32 PM

Whether goodness or badness is the better gift option depends on social circumstances and perspective glances.

<u>On Sounded Steps</u> 12/25/2024 09:35 PM

Dance and let the moment declare quality.

<u>On Word Timing</u> 12/25/2024 09:36 PM

Whether to reveal or conceal is a tricky business governed by time and circumstances.

<u>On Human Frailty</u> 12/26/2024 01:54 AM

Like pains, some flaws can be hidden and some remain visible.

<u>On Reasoning Flaws</u> 12/27/2024 02:48 PM

Reasoning relies on fact-based perspective and perspective can be manipulated.

<u>On Time is Money</u> 12/27/2024 02:57 PM

Time is money means more than just ties to currency. It also means physical, mental, and emotional expenditures.

<u>On Compunction Feels</u> 12/27/2024 03:00 PM

Free the mind and the tongue begs to follow the same course, sometimes coarsely.

<u>On Thinking Pokes</u> 12/27/2024 05:11 PM

Rational growth sometimes spreads wild as weeds.

<u>On Perception Perspective</u> 12/29/2024 12:15 PM

Enjoy truth for as long as it can last or laugh.

<u>On Fated Moments</u> 12/29/2024 PM 12:19

For every measured month and date there is an hour and minute at a specific place. Each building block of one's life is portrayed there. It could be mainly one place or many over time. A legacy of senses and sensations molds the character.

<u>On Journalism Millionaires</u> 12/29/2024 02:38 PM

Rachel Maddow is a broom flying, gaslighting, narcissistic, mirror breaking , bowling alley balloon popper. Happy Maddow Day!

<u>On Resource Management</u> 12/29/2024 04:24 PM

Minimize the use of resources. You never know when they may become unavailable, useless, outdated, or cease to exist.

<u>On Nature's Nature</u> 12/29/2024 04:26 PM

Nature is a one-sided acquaintance.

<u>On Human Species Earth Inhabitance</u> 12/29/2024 07:13 PM

Of all animal species on this planet earth, only humans have a mental capacity to survive and reside in every corner of and continent of it. The humans are also the youngest animal species. We are basically still crawling around in the playpen compared to all other species.

<u>Shadows Within My Mind</u> on Facebook 12/29/2024 08:00 PM

"All roads lead to you, even those I took to forget you." Mahoud Darwish

"If you only read the books that everyone else is reading, you can only think what everyone else is thinking." Haruki Murakami

<u>On Human Frailty</u> 12/31/2024 01:26 PM

Too many humans are basically comparable to puke. And too, many of those pukes hold positions of power.

<u>On Depravity Reigns</u> 12/31/2024 01:34 PM

The evil-doers are allowed, in too many societies, to quash the do-gooders far too much. The law and laws have never stopped being a jackass.

<u>On Perception Errors</u> 01/01/2025 03:10 AM

There is no single experience of perspective that contributes to accurate perceptions. Flaws abide everywhere in the human mind calculation and process subconsciously; conspire with the bits and pieces of the past, present, and future calculations to produce inaccuracies. All of the working human senses incidentally contribute to formative rational conclusions while rationing somewhat randomly the quality level of each sense moment's significance. Furthermore, the present state of mind whether dour or joyful will trifle idly during the battles of thought processes ignited. Thus, the mind draws a map almost haplessly seeking to make sure a destination conclusion can be sighted. Lo and behold, human misery and loathing of the result becomes tossed away like garbage or hailed as souvenir salvation. Every concept, evolution of thoughts, practice of deeds, existences passed on replicates this random unwholesome wheel of process, and has mechanically churned along for 2 million years and counting.

On Trust Rules 01/01/2025 04:57 PM

What? There are rules? Of course there are rules. The trust tower can be easily felled by a single instance of infidelity.

On Politics 01/02/2025 02:59 PM

There is no such thing as an honest politician. Essentially, honest politicians are based on myth.

On Humors of Humans 01/02/2025 03:16 PM

Despite the bleak, overly competitive human existence messes, made so by human leaders themselves, a simple laugh and timely words, and a sensical humor, picks well the lighter strings of life.

On Soul Roads 01/03/2025 03:32 AM

There are times in life when the soul wants to fly to another place, and there are times when the soul must find a way while chained in place.

On Writing 01/03/2025 07:56 PM

A simple arrangement, no more than necessary, creates a story of enlightening sequences made worthy of a read.

On Sometimes Misguided 01/03/2025 08:08 PM

Sometimes one must dispossess from the company of others who offered much for one's own benefit.

On Power Trips 01/04/2025 01:11 PM

Power is greedy for more power until it finds it must destroy the selfish nature of itself to survive.

On Government Overreach 01/05/2025 02:48 PM

Government desires to rule over anything and everything.

On Measures Great and Small 01/05/2025 02:50 PM

The ruler measures. The Ruler treasures.

On Accurate 01/05/2025 02:53 PM

Preciseness is many times a life-or-death matter.

On Writing 01/05/2025 02:58 PM

Throw a lot of words on the page. Watch them mingle at the Story Ball. Much can happen during the reader's mind of the dance.

On Prophecy Pokes 01/05/2025 03:00 PM

Words create pictures. Pictures create words. A dichotomy rich.

On Music 01/05/2025 03:03 PM

Thank you so much for existing.

On Humankind 01/05/2025 03:13 PM

Neglected by the universe at large, ungrateful recipients of random gifts betrothed by the elements, disrespectful towards themselves and each other, their worth has yet to display any viable measure of need or purpose. Not judgment. Just an observation.

On Creativity 01/05/2025 03:19 PM

A mythical projection of harmony in reality much needed to fuel the human engine.

On Hatred Miscues 01/05/2025 03:24 PM

Don't hate humans. They hate themselves more than enough.

On News Happy 01/05/2025 03:25 PM

If you want a happy ending, then read a romantic fairy tale.

On Snowstorms 01/05/2025 03:28 PM

A beautiful picture of and for destruction. A very pretty blanket of potential doom.

On Get Togethers 01/05/2025 04:07 PM

When a meeting of minds fails to occur then a static infection grows.

On Thinking 01/05/2025 08:43 PM

Reason is the season, and that season should exist

all year long.

On Random Thought Sparks 01/07/2025 01:18 PM ? Fractillion Infarction ? ? Armra Makeup / Cosmetics Remover ?

On Government Hypocrisy 01/07/2025 07:20 PM

In California, why does every season remind me of the last days of the ancient Roman Empire?

On Routine Choices 01/08/2025 01:04 PM

Rushing into the next moment is a product of habit. Keep up with "so and so" to get that "thing" done. Such a condition isn't living a life. Such a condition is a social poison immorally injected into the body politic. Ask who injects such poison and why. The answers will determine the master. Then, ask is it necessary to serve that master.

On Learning 01/08/2025 04:14 PM

Understanding is not a natural human condition. It must be learned through exertion of mind and body.

On Wants 01/09/2025 03:00 AM

Satisfaction is overrated.

On Aging 01/09/2025 03:03 AM

Young boy days fade in the haze.

On Leadership Matters 01/09/2025 04:03 AM

Whoever leads the crowd orchestrates the madness that ensues.

On Rare Moments Random 01/09/2025 04:08 AM

An exchange of a glance can create an emotion ping that gongs like a temple bell depending on the circumstances.

On Severing Ties 01/09/2025 02:12 PM

We've been taught to follow our elders and get along with the crowd. We're not born civilized. Observationally, much knowledge can be gained during this process, but know that such a journey isn't a commitment. It's a free-will path.

On Captured Life 01/09/2025 02:23 PM

We're born into essentially closed social cultures. At some future point, the individual mind must decide the benefits and detriments of limiting their lives to only the tenets espoused in that society.

On Lovers Leaps 01/10/2025 03:41 AM

Experience amongst mutual lovers implies other lovers may exist in the same village, town, city, or other places. Reasons vary for compatibility whether necessary, convenient, or perhaps born of somewhat intersessional or desperation fears.

On Taxation Machinations 01/10/2025 03:57 AM

If a fairly elected government really cared about citizens, then it wouldn't tax them into financial servitude. Taxation is a form of theft and enslavement. The same principle applies to government spending demands.

On Schrodinger's Cat 01/10/2025 01:49 PM

Basically, the universe is the box.

On Economics Theory 01/10/2025 01:54 PM

Every creature on planet earth is a capitalist.

Shadows Within My Mind on Facebook 01/10/2025 02:01 PM

"He who dares not offend cannot be honest." Thomas Paine

Science & Technology on Facebook 01/11/2025 05:36 PM "A great many people think they are thinking when they are merely rearranging their prejudices." William James

On Soul Theory 01/12/2025 12:53 AM

The soul takes its energy from emotions, therefore, the concept of it is an emotion. To lack a soul is not to literally die.

01:23 AM

The lack is a quirk in the emotional system. Need to master the emotional engine of the soul to become a better benevolent human.

02:41 AM

The soul is an emotion so it can only emote.

<u>On Heartrending</u> 01/12/2024 04:35 AM

A sound emanating more frequently, or a heart spiritually or physically feeling great or gratis pain?

<u>On Studies Perspective</u> 01/12/2025 03:59 PM

Scientists, politicians, journalists are paid to lie.

<u>On What Imagination is Made of</u> 01/12/2025 11:59 PM

Pixie dust and salacious rust.

<u>On Sleep Cycles Unordinary</u> 01/13/2025 05:50 AM Sometimes I couldn't sleep at night. Really, I almost always couldn't sleep. The internal clock didn't want to cooperate with the city folks clock or the farmers clock. I would still be awake, occasionally getting out of bed in the range of 3 AM to 6 AM, often looking out the bedroom window. My mind seemed to wait for something to appear or pass by during or near pre-dawn hours. A fox, deer, rats, rabbits tended to a similar cycle, including some birds like the finches, bluejays, and cardinals depending on the season.

The house, walls, ceiling snored, stretched, wrestled around as if in a dream state, too, during the aforementioned hours. During these times the local classical music radio station summoned forth sounds spanning the past 400 years melodies and harmonies composed of genius minds. The sounds represented thoughts, emotions, dreams. Even now my mind is unwilling to be constrained by the hour of a day. It's a human made structure not accommodative to my internal clock nature.

<u>On Tragedies Political</u> 01/13/2025 03:14 PM Media calls the California fires "L. A. fires" when they should more accurately call it "Politician Fires".

<u>On Poisons Political</u> 01/13/2025 03:16 PM

If citizens, in self-defense, had the right to kill those who stole the most money and property from them, then most of those killed would be politicians.

<u>On Religion</u> 01/13/2025 04:40 PM

Religion is largely a cultural and political fraud designed to exercise control over the populace it is applied to. No more, no less.

<u>On Biden Truth</u> 01/13/2025 04:45 PM

The Biden administration touted pseudo-truth. Essentially, selling a bag of popcorn scorched black during the cooking process. Inedible.

<u>On Government Machinations</u> 01/13/2025 05:41 PM

Every government entity is a marketeer, and their major weapon is media propaganda.

<u>On Truth Forges</u> 01/13/2025 05:59 PM

Truth, so difficult to discern and confirm, can be either a dull or sharp blade, but also many times is forged in the fires of fantasy.

<u>On Physical Earth</u> 01/13/2025 06:02 PM

The environment is unforgiving, supported by those who have become conspirators with it.

<u>On California Dreaming</u> 01/13/2025 07:30 PM

Gavin Newsom will forever be known as the Los Angeles angel of death.

<u>On Book Bakes</u> 01/13/2025 07:39 PM

A novel is like a cake with a lot of words and meanings baked into it.

<u>Shadows Within My Mind</u> on Facebook 01/14/2025 03:35 PM

"Maybe all one can do is hope to end up with the right regrets."
Arthur Miller

On Government 01/15/2025 02:37 PM

Class tier defines freedom in every governmental system.

On Public Services 01/15/2025 05:55 PM

There should be a mandatory law applied to all USA jurisdictions renaming and labeling outdoor public use trashcans as a "Bidenbin".

On California Dreaming 01/15/2025 10:10 PM

The California wildfires are what happens when human natural disasters are elected into political office. Citizens might want to consider not electing politicians who are literally killing them.

On Totalitarian Society 01/15/2025 11:11 PM

Every society has wretched offshoots, and some of those offshoots shoot indiscriminately.

On Philosophy Tenets 01/16/2025 03:02 PM

The philosopher's purpose is to share tenets of everyday life known, then to seek the knowledge of what is not shown but can be discovered and shared amongst the masses of humanity for consideration.

On Moments' Longevity 01/16/2025 04:18 PM

Don't throw away moments. It is like throwing away seedlings.

On Media Mania 01/16/2025 04:53 PM

A staple of the unstable human media communicators is lack a proper perspective. Generally, they've demonstrated an instability exemplified by using words to fling rotten corn cobs. The Queen of Hearts mindset lives to persecute Alice for as long as Alice lives on whichever side of the mirror inhabited.

On Dirt 01/16/2025 06:52 PM

What we step upon every day in the outdoors world serves valuable meaning and purpose. Dirt. It reveals solemn serenity; exposes the wind for what it is; feeds the environment's natural need for sustenance.

On Time Waiting 01/17/2025 12:34 AM

Time consumes all by any measurable means. How much time in our lives do we use up waiting? Possible time consumption: observation of immediate surroundings; contemplation of a previous task held in the mind's "to do" bin; memory resurrections; immediate future time usage and necessity. Perhaps, bring a book, magazine, or mobile phone, just in case the time loops planned a trip up or down unexpectedly.

On Reality Clay 01/17/2025 02:07 PM Much of what we believe is reality beams out as propagandized fiction, at least in how a perception of reality is portrayed then consumed. Marketers, politicians, and media outlets twist and mold reality perceptions. Fiction for profit. Reality sprinkles optional.

On Fact Bonding 01/17/2025 02:36 PM

Facts are the glue that binds reality bits. When facts are faked or flawed through lies, deceits, or mistakes then reality becomes blasted into little pieces unbound.

On Deviant Falsehoods 01/17/2025 02:38 PM

Fraud is a lie presented as truth.

On Existence Sparks 01/17/2025 02:39 PM

You are alive. Make it count.

On Human Resurrections 01/17/2025 02:42 PM

Embrace your mistakes. They are a sacred teaching tool. Once the lesson is learned, let the mistakes dissolve into the mists of time, but remember the lesson.

On AI Pumping 01/17/2025 02:45 PM If the wrong graded fuel mixture is pumped into an automotive vehicle, then the vehicle will gradually break down.

Shadows Within My Mind on Facebook 01/17/2025 04:36 PM

"To read without reflecting, is like eating without digestion." Edmund Burke

"Motivation is overrated, environment often matters more." James Clear, Atomic Habits

<u>On Art Smart</u> 01/18/2025 04:02 AM

The art of any activity is to exercise creatively without releasing a fart.

<u>On Memories Aged</u> 01/18/2025 04:10 AM

Life's memories become so distorted over time that their paths seem questionable. Grape or Tomato?

<u>On Organization Bonds</u> 01/19/2025 02:28 AM

The lowest common denominator of any hierarchy system is discrimination in the form of nepotism.

<u>On Marriage Vows</u> 01/19/2025 02:31 AM Good intentions sometimes evolve into struggles unsolvable. Forever just isn't a very long time.

<u>On Government Vows</u> 01/19/2025 02:33 AM

Fiction is threaded into and across any painted canvas.

<u>On Religion Tenets</u> 01/19/2025 02:35 AM

A purse often stolen and rummaged through by the hungry dog's emotions.

<u>On Youthful Dangers Faced</u> 01/19/202502:39 AM

Growing up involves many moments of running away and hiding until the danger passes.

<u>On Rotting Inevitable</u> 01/19/2025 02:44 AM

Food sources are like life fazes and forms. They rot away if not timely consumed.

<u>On Evolutionary Principles</u> 01/19/2025 02:51 AM

Existence is not a static affair, nor is knowledge accumulation.

<u>On the Human Mind</u> 01/19/2025 03:00 AM

Is the universe an artificial intelligence (AI) mechanism designed to make sense of itself? Is that circumstance singularity? No human has ever reached singularity. Intelligence is fungible and often questionable.

On Shipping and Handling 01/19/2025 04:19 AM

Grip is everything in many ways.

On Genes Data 01/19/2025 04:36 AM

If our birthed genes connect us to our family history, then do they also connect us to a subconscious storage bin of the memories held by our ancestors? Are dreams revealing a past history of more than our own experiences but also those of our deceased elders?

Scientists surmise humans use on 20 percent of their brain matter capacity. Parts of it are either dormant or not yet activated during an entire lifetime. The future development of the non-functional parts of the human brain may hold or mask past family or genetic memories which we've not yet evolved enough to experience all at once, just as a library which houses thousands of books. Only one book can be read at a time. And reading is not necessarily understanding. Comprehension involves many steps, including storage ability of data consumption.

Individual brains do not operate in a collective manner. Shared knowledge depends on many elements including consumption and digestion of it, understanding what has been consumed, sharing it with others, and each of these steps potentially involve misinterpretation, improper filtering such a bias or prejudice. Each connection involves a crooked nail hammered into rotted wood. Just a few rotted building blocks weakens the integrity of the dwelling.

On Singularity 01/19/2025 02:50 PM

To know is a tentative concept built on research and scientific testing. To know everything about anything is also a tentative concept. Singularity is not possible. The resulting nuances are endless in possibilities. Possibility is the glue that holds together facts and faith. None of each is written in stone, or an unbreakable tenet of existence. Singularity is not possible logically.

<u>Shadows Within My Mind</u> on Facebook 01/19/2025 04:30 PM

"Every child is an artist, the problem is how to remain an artist once he grows." Pablo Picasso

"One child, one teacher, one book, one pen and change the world." Malada Yousafzai

"Rest, nature, books, music, such is my idea of happiness." Leo Tolstoy

<u>On Mystic Thoughts</u> 01/19/2025 05:33 PM

"Science without religion is lame. Religion without science is blind." Albert Einstein

<u>President 47's First 100 Days Begins</u>

<u>On Misplaced Trust</u> 01/20/2025 02:52 PM

There's one thing in life I've learned astoundingly and resoundingly: never trust a politician.

<u>On Time Sounds</u> 01/21/2025 04:58 AM

Sometimes music combines with sounds and words as if birthed by outer space and time rhythms. Ex: Vivaldi, Mozart Chopin, Dvorak, Led Zeppelin, Pink Floyd, Aerosmith, Def Leppard

<u>On Viewpoint 01/21/2025 05:49 PM</u>

Perspective and prejudice are two sides of the same coin.

<u>Shadows Within My Mind</u> on Facebook 01/25/2025 05:59 PM

"It's strange. I felt less lonely when I didn't know you." Jean Paul Sartre

"Unlimited power in the hands of limited people always leads to cruelty." Aleksandr Solzhenitsyn

<u>On Changes</u> 01/22/2025 01:57 AM

Missing someone hurts, so the best that could happen is you stop missing them, if the hurt feels too bad. Remember this lesson.

<u>On Fleeting Follies</u> 01/22/2025 05:04 AM

For every up there's a down. For every smile there's a frown. Jokers and clowns abound.

<u>On Sleep Neediness</u> 01/22/2025 05:08 AM

In youth, sleep is a chore. In elder age it is a bore.

<u>On the Dimension Connections</u> 01/22/2025 03:38 PM

If the dimension has an entrance and exit point, just like a store or residence, and given the distances of dimension to/from those points, then all knowledge and experience has intersected across this universe and beyond, meaning all of these places have been affected and effected during interactions. Culture and environment in this existence holds elements shared by contact and extension.

Many humans and other creatures have already traveled to and from these locations in dreams, is a possible supposition astrally in the form of astral projection. The ignition of dreams during sleep is not specifically known. It is supposed that they originate from current extant encounters. What if they are inherited ignitions? A means of collecting genetic information which ignites past family incidents in long ago time periods. A difficult factor to manage in my own dream experiences is whether the dream is based on physical reality experiences or inspired by much of the reading I've done over 60 years.

<u>On Internet Lessons</u> 01/22/2025 03:49 PM

Internet access has taught us how and why humans can't be trusted, not even for one second. Discretion may be the better part of valor, and so to it is the better part of education and learning.

<u>On Perception</u> 01/22/2025 03:55 PM

Never presume honesty. It is presented in pretty and glitzy packages, but hides purpose.

<u>On Words Necessary</u> 01/22/2025 04:49 PM

The words "shit turd" is emphatically redundant, applicable to any corrupt human. Useable as complementary nouns, pronouns, adjectives, adverbs, verbs.

<u>On Meals</u> 01/22/2025 07:50 PM

Some workers eat meals at breakfast, lunch, dinner, and snack times based on their work hours. Lundin is a combo of lunch and dinner which some cultures combine into one meal moment. Much like the brunch, a combination of breakfast and lunch. Perhaps these mealtime combinations are necessary for convenience and efficiency in the daily life cycle.

<u>On Quantum Particle Theory</u> 01/23/2025 04:15 AM

Much of quantum physics remains in the theoretical stage despite media efforts to portray it as currently tested, viable, and useful. Many puzzle pieces are missing in this advocacy and marketing propaganda phase.

Think of this phase as the process of completing a puzzle from scratch. The cardboard pieces must be connected to see the whole picture. Puzzle solving involves finding first the outer pieces which reveal themselves by outer "edge" portions and "corner" portions.

Quantum Particle theory is still a puzzle with an inadequate number of edge and corner pieces. The middle pieces, if they exist, can't be connected without a frame of containment. The theory jumps and bounces around randomly like the middle puzzle pieces' space slots looking for a proper placement. It is possible that completion of this puzzle turns off the universe as we currently and insufficiently know.

<u>On Gender Twists</u> 01/23/2025 06:32 PM

Gender identity is a leftist stink bomb.

<u>On Government Excess</u> 01/23/2025 06:50 PM

Governments openly display an insatiable lust for taxpayers' money.

<u>On Bullseyes</u> 01/23/2025 07:15 PM

Nonsense hates when verbal daggers are tossed at it.

<u>On Media Entertainment</u> 01/23/2025 08:06 PM

While watching what we used to call "TV", I often think "dumbasses" and "asses dumber".

<u>On Short Stories</u> 01/24/2025 01:54 AM

"The Kid"

A little boy was born with a mental deficiency, allowing his mind and body to become a self-defense weapon as compensation. This conclusion was determined by a school counselor based on the circumstances investigated to date. During the initial interview, counselor noted the boy's physical acts of shivering and clasping hands together to cover his face at first, but later to jam his hands under his armpits. The counselor determined the boy suffered a fear, essentially, of everything.

An investigation of the boy's father and other family members learned the story of how, as a baby, the boy was almost kidnapped by a mysterious and only partially visible entity. Further investigation determined the entity form as an upper body torso type of organism able to float on and control gravity.

The counselor was suspicious about such a story and description. Police records revealed no reports of such an incident. The counselor wondered why the father and family members never mentioned the boy's mother. He checked school records to identify the mother. The records indicated "Mother: unknown". The physical place of the birth was also unknown.

Continued counseling sessions with the boy determined the boy was afraid of himself, too. The father told the counselor during follow up home visits about strange occurrences at night. The boy would be noted as missing after being put to bed, but only for a few hours before returning.

The counselor noticed a portion of the home property abutted a thick line of trees and bushes. He went in amongst them and discovered dead animals and animals remains. Creatures like squirrels, rodents, birds, and even an empty turtle that seemed empty, frozen in place on the ground as if they were displayable knick-knacks.

Oddly, no death aroma emanated from them. No signs of blood or scavenged flesh. Near some of the animals were only piles of dark-colored sandy clumps. All of these dead creatures and clumps seemed impervious to wind currents. Leaves would blow around and above them but never touch upon them. Not a single spot of ground or sky detritus were attached to them.

The counselor determined some outdoor exercise might be appropriate for the boy during school break periods and cleared the idea with the school principal. The first visit confirmed a lot of the information developed to date. The boy seemed unfazed or moved by the walk through of the area just a few feet into the thinly lined tree growth at the edge of the school playground. The counselor noticed animals in a similar condition as the scene he had observed near the boy's home. The boy seemed accustomed to such a sight. The notion that a similarity to the home and school areas seemed more than coincidental. Two animal death sights at the locations the boy mainly experienced life concerned the counselor.

The boy and counselor continued somewhat regular visits to both sites so the counselor could witness any unusual interactions between the boy and nature life. At the first such observed encounter, just the sounds of noises in the tree line frightened the boy. He seemed overly concerned and tense. The counselor explained there was nothing to fear. It was then a squirrel showed itself creeping downward along a nearby tree trunk. The boy froze in place, his eyes closed.

The squirreled dissolved into dust about 6 feet from the ground. No detritus entered the atmosphere randomness. The dust frost into place against the tree trunk appearing as a mini-pyramid object. The boy opened his eyes, walked over to the tree, extended his left hand palm up and pretended to press his hand against the object, not touching it, just focused on the spot. After about ten seconds, the mini-pyramid appeared to solidify as if permanently connected to the tree all along. The counselor became nervous, not knowing what to say or do, if anything was required to do. He didn't want to enhance the boy's fear, now realizing to do so could heighten the boys fear. No words were exchanged and each of them left the scene together.

On their next meeting together at the counselor's school office, he recommended the boy keep a written journal of similar experiences, advising to do so may help the boy understand himself better. The counselor also advised it may be a good idea not to discuss their sessions with anyone until the counselor could help the boy understand the events they experienced together. The boy agreed. The counselor also requested he be allowed to review the journal entries to help the boy understand what had happened and what might happen in the future. He agreed, stating his family didn't understand it and was unable to offer him help in understanding.

The next week another school counseling session proceeded, and the counselor read the boy's journal. It made no suggestion of any similar incidents. The counselor asked what were the boy's activities that week. The boy stated he had come to school, a short walk, and had gone home. Nothing else, except homework, and writing in the journal. The counselor asked if the boy had entered the tree line at home or school. The boy answered no. The session ended at the regular time.

The counselor reviewed the journal again after the boy left the office. He determined he should revisit each tree line site to determine if any more incidents had occurred that perhaps the boy felt ashamed or worried about and failed to include them. Upon a visit to each place, councilor discovered similar frozen animals and dust piles. A few more counseling sessions were completed. The journal read accounts of almost the exact same routine as previous entries. No real deviation. No mention of frozen creatures or dust piles.

The counselor wondered if the boy had been born with neural problems which caused his mind to hide instances of fear as an emotional defense mechanism. The counselor's next step was to investigate the boy's family history. Checked local records, school records, property records, internet sites looking for available potential evidence sources and further leads. He was able to determine the family had a gypsy ethnic heritage. In that heritage exists many stories and ancient legends about family interactions with nature, varied environments, adaptability physical and economic survival measures the group followed and implemented.

He discovered numerous implemented actions this society enacted to continue existence. Many of the methods involved casting spells to shield their presence in the landscape where they lived and manipulate nature around them for protection. A common element of these defense systems involved altering the existing environment which included methods like the counselor encountered at the tree lined site. These manipulations involve more than objects. They included manipulation of animal life such as creating spice scents that would attract or repel certain creatures depending on food, monetary benefits, or need or physical defense perimeters. He was astounded to find an instance when a bear was used as an ornamental addition to the community perimeter in order to scare away any intruders. Instructions were included about how to paralyze the bear, then preserve it in a jelly-like cover. Essentially, a type of modern-day taxidermy.

The counselor began to wonder if the boy was being trained in this method to help his family protect itself whenever it moved to a different location. Then a flash of thought struck the counselor. Was the family teaching the boy personal, physical self-defense methods to avoid harm infliction during encounters with others around him? There were no reported instances of bullying inflicted upon him at school. No history of past bullying. Perhaps the boy was able to temporarily defend himself with an emotion fueled physical shield. The boy used physical actions to freeze a squirrel, stop it in its tracks, or to completely neutralize one permanently by turning it into dust.

As a last consideration, the counselor wondered is the father was intentionally omitting his knowledge about the mother, either to protect his and her reputation at the time, or to conceal a power she had to manipulate life in creatures small and larger, perhaps even human control mastery. Perhaps it was the custom of a gypsy group to conceal their most powerful members to prevent attempts by outsiders from trying to destroy that power, then weaken or destroy the gypsy group to acquire their knowledge and resources.

The counselor concluded that he had solved the mystery. Although the boy didn't speak much he apparently listened well and long. He could do two things rather well: read fast, and make notes about much of what he listened to, perhaps to perform research on the topic for further knowledge development later. Those notes the boy never shared with the counselor. One of the teachers at school revealed the boy had often requested another pencil because he had worn down the tip so much, he needed to make regular visits to use the pencil sharpener.

The counselor still had some questions which needed answers. When the boy didn't show up for the next counseling session, he visited the principal's office to inquire about it. The principal didn't know why and suggested another visit to the boy's home. Upon the counselor's visit to the home, a knock on the front door received no answer so he walked around the property a bit and found a real estate agent assessing the property. She revealed the family had moved out unexpectedly. The father had previously notified a neighbor about the move and asked the neighbor to inform the landlord. The counselor walked away wondering how the boy and his family were doing. Hoped all was okay. While driving away he noticed the mailbox on a post at the end of the dirt road driveway was half opened. He stopped and saw a while envelope.

Out of curiosity he reached inside and found a yellow envelope, unsealed, addressed only to "counselor". He found inside it a journal book just like one the boy presented to him during counseling sessions, although much more weathered in appearance. Opening the book showed notes written in what appeared stenography notations. He drove to the courthouse and asked if he was correct. A court stenographer agreed it was in facts stenography.

The counselor feared what the stenographer would read, so he thanked him and then drove back to the school office to determine the best way to proceed. Perhaps, the best way was to not proceed further. One thing he was sure of. He needed to learn stenography.

<u>On Emotions</u> 01/24/2025 03:11 AM

Happiness is fleeting. Hold on as long as possible.

<u>On Cultural Demise</u> 01/24/2025 02:24 PM

A culture is made up of people civil and kind, and also people grinding away at taking everything at any cost or amount of damage. I attribute such situations to how a society treats citizens, and further, to how society educates children. Too many roadblocks. Not enough finished roadwork.

<u>On Political Mayhem</u> 01/24/2025 04:58 PM

The Democrat Party seems dedicated to turning our country into a freak show of mayhem, perhaps because such a condition turns eyes away from Democrat Pary money laundering scams.

On Media Chicanery 01/24/2025 05:09 PM Favoritism or nepotism isn't a constitutional offense but using lies to intentionally deceive (democratism) citizens in a caustic harmful manner sabotages the constitutional rights of all people.

On Elemental Physics 01/26/2025 02:03 AM

Freak shows +/- irrational insanity = reality to the nth power.

On Reality Bits 01/26/2025 03:24 AM

If every day wasn't challenging, then it wouldn't mimic real life.

On Coincidence 01/26/2025 03:46 AM

If you're living, then you're also dreaming.

On Burdens Bland 01/26/2025 03:49 AM

If lightness is darkness, then darkness is lightness.

On Temperance Traps 01/26/2025 03:51 PM

Freedom is an entrapment of simple minds when the modern-day synonym becomes wokeness.

On Language Puzzling 01/26/2025 03:53 AM

Too many meanings, not enough words. Too many words, not enough meanings.

On Natures Angles 01/26/2025 03:55 AM

Climate is a bastard searching for a bitch.

On Estates 01/26/2025 03:58 AM

Real estate is a fiction and affectation of ego.

On Merry Movement 01/26/2025 04:00 AM

An active reasonable mind is an engine finely tuned.

On Spasm Ham 01/26/2025 04:02 PM

What else is there to do but everything? (I actually asked a Manager this question on one of my jobs. His brain went sproing. I was the only one working while others were loafing. One of the loafers was his son. Naturally, my pay was docked.)

<u>On Sweet Paths</u> 01/26/2025 04:04 AM

Music soothes soles of feet and souls of mind.

<u>On Chaotic Karma</u> 01/26/2025 04:08 AM

Too many sounds. Not enough silence.

<u>On Task Terrors</u> 01/26/2025 04:09

Get it done or bury it. Seems to be a government mantra.

<u>On Space Anywhere</u> 01/26/2025 04:12 AM

Atomically, all life forms and objects are alive to some degree macroscopically and microscopically.

<u>On Infinity</u> 01/26/2025 04:15 AM

All of existence creates further existence. Infinity is a fiction when conceived as a physical place.

<u>On Folly Notices</u> 01/26/2025 04:18

History is a footnote in the book of existence. We know much less than we don't know. And what we know has often been misrepresented based on perspective and prejudice.

<u>On figuring it out</u> 01/26/2025 04:21 AM

Mind sparks create meaning both valid and unvalued if not questionable in totem.

<u>On It Id</u> 01/26/2025 04:23 AM

Not doing anything means still doing something. The universe never rests.

<u>On Doldrums Productive</u> 01/26/2025 04:26 AM

A lazy haze daze played out in waves.

<u>On Activity Unlimited</u> 01/26/2025 04:30 AM

There's no such thing as chasing nothing in the animal world.

<u>On Commonality</u> 01/26/2025 04:32 AM

Awake and asleep serve the same purpose.

<u>On Inner Calm</u> 01/26/2025 04:34 AM

Zen banishes rational fears. Seems a bit dangerous.

<u>On Circles Curious</u> 01/26/2025 04:39 AM

Singularity is the tale of an animal chasing its tale.

Or, the tale of an animal chasing a tale of an animal.

<u>On Bait & Hitch</u> 01/26/2025 04:44 AM

A confused mind is something like a hooked fish.

<u>On Artificial Intelligence</u> 01/26/2025 04:49 AM

A computerized intelligence can only produce knowledge and misconception portrayed from the program source materials. Consuming it is comparable to consuming the wax apple in the real estate agent's model house dining table.

<u>On Magic Science</u> 01/26/2025 05:03 AM

The human body is a suitcase full of ancient biological magic tricks.

<u>On Personal Wishes</u> 01/26/2025 06:26 AM

May happy moments outnumber sad moments.

<u>On Careful Moves</u> 01/26/2025 06:37 AM

We trick ourselves into adopting certain mind sets in order to tread life's stairs and steps safely.

<u>On Writer's Life</u> 01/26/2025 06:40 AM

Living is a small price to pay compared to penning words upon the pad page.

<u>On Literature gods</u> 01/26/2025 06:42 AM

Writers serve readers. Readers are the gods of a written work's worth and viability.

<u>On Love's Pesters</u> 01/26/2025 06:44 AM

Memories of previous love relationships keep me awake at night, and asleep during dreams. Fortunately, an escapable curse.

<u>On Muse Soundings</u> 01/26/2025 06:46 AM

There is no music as mesmerizing and stimulating as the sounds of nature.

<u>On Life Living Cycles</u> 01/26/2025 06:58 AM Commence days' time life, commence. The morning's shroud has been lifted. Commence nights' time life, commence. The evening's shroud has been lifted.

<u>On Destiny's Search</u> 01/27/2025 05:57AM

In order to find a path for your life, it helps to take a figurative walk and begin the search. Destiny is not assigned at birth. It must be earned.

<u>On Energy Drains</u> 01/27/2025 06:03 AM The time to rest is debatable but necessary.

<u>On Political Observations</u> 01/27/2025 12:33 PM

An accurate description of some politicians is "a walkin' talkin' mouth shitter."

<u>On AFC Championship Summary</u> 01/27/2025 02:50 PM

The NFL story headline should read "KC Thiefs Steal Another Win Officiated by English Premier League trained Refs".

<u>On Mild Flowers</u> 01/28/2025 04:24 AM

When the point of an argument ends up being pointless then the purpose reigns as passive dismissive in wilting moments of time.

<u>On Vows Crooked</u> 01/28/2025 04:27 AM

Once in a lifetime lasts as short or long as a marriage.

<u>On Sporting Communications</u> 01/28/2025 04:30 AM

Some passings of knowledge are blocked, topped, fumbled, dropped, or intercepted.

<u>On Reality Bents</u> 01/28/2025 04:42 AM

The universe either is or is not. Or, maybe both flexibly.

<u>On Garden Grows</u> 01/28/2025 04:55 AM

In the weeds of doubt hide the seeds of guilt.

<u>On Chance Mystery</u> 01/28/2025 04:00 PM

An opportunity is often not such.

<u>On Learning-Zings</u> 01/28/2025 04:13 PM

Humans have had 300,000 years to figure out what is humanity, and they haven't figured it out yet.

On NFL Fans 01/28/2025 04:29 PM

The NFL is both a sports and social organization. It brings together elite athletes from every corner of the globe permitting the world to help gain a perspective about life and humanity interactions on the football field. This sports organization's competitions provide insights into everyday social interactions of fans, for fans, and about fans. Essentially, fans can become select members of the NFL organization as a Team, worker, player, owner, fan. The fans off the field and in stadium stands evolve in amazing ways in the mind and heart.

For instance, the Baltimore Ravens and Pittsburgh Steelers players and fans are portrayed as enemies and eternal rivals. The same relationship is not applicable to matchups between the same groups of Buffalo Bills and Baltimore Ravens despite hotly contested games in their playoff matchups. Win or lose, during or after matchups, a unique and mysterious bond has evolved amongst each Team's fans and players, perhaps assisted by game competitions. Fans and players of these Teams have formed a bond that connects them to life's purer humanity notions, financially helping injured players either physically through words or deeds, spiritually in proper sentiments, or charitably in monetary contributions.

On Fungible Society 01/28/2025 06:22 PM Love is as fungible as any other existence element.

On Government Cleansing 01/28/2025 08:18 PM

Now that the Biden administration has been excised from the political landscape, one week later the U.S. citizen desire for liberty and justice has risen, to near flood water levels needed to cleanse the lands of propaganda hoaxes and money laundering crimes. An absolute and swift cleaning continues in DOGE earnest.

<u>On Words Audible in Unusual Places</u> 01/28/2025 10:50 PM

The longer or more frequent each is away from human influences, the more non-human creatures and inanimate objects seem to be attempting mutually beneficial communications.

<u>On Government's Purpose</u> 01/29/2025 07:43 PM

Governments are freely elected to serve the citizens and not serve themselves. Any deviation from this sacred promise is cause for revolution. Excise the scoundrels who prefer slavery.

<u>On Government Considerations</u> 01/29/2025 07:48 PM Government should necessarily fear the existence of a law abiding citizen.

<u>On Political Cycle Courses</u> 01/29/2025 08:04 PM

Magazine "Vogue" isn't in vogue as ankle biters.

<u>On Journalism Ethics</u> 01/29/2025 09:36 PM

Too many journalists: immoral as the day is long.

<u>On A Space-Time Prayer</u> 01/30/2025 03:41 AM

In reality as we've learned, the will of a human mind was shaped by violent subjugation. Only the physically and mentally adept and strong maintained absolute control. Progress came through those in power maintained by any means possible. The subjugated knew no free will concept. Such a mentality myth persisted. Then, the tiniest of creatures microscopic controlled human destiny over a life daily subjected to the confines of imminent death.

Science knowledge and chemical discoveries have helped humans cheat imminent death temporarily. Nature is the only god on land, the above, and the below. But now another god has entered the picture. Another man-created god called artificial intelligence (AI), fueled by scientific advancements (Quantum Mechanics, Quantum Computing). The purpose of these new gods is no different than the ancient human creation of the mythical gods: to control humans. Amen.

<u>On Media Quality</u> 01/30/2025 10:53 AM

Media integrity is an oxymoron.

<u>On Political Reality</u> 01/30/2025 11:14 AM

The U.S. Democrat Party is a white elephant.

<u>On Political Nominees</u> 01/31/2025 12:04 AM

When watching the President Trump Executive Branch nominations, it became crystal clear what a bunch of scoundrels and sore losers inhabit the Democrat Party political world. Appalling from any reasonable perspective. No class, no decorum offered. Just trash talk.

<u>On My "Thinker" Story</u> 01/31/2025 03:18 PM

I'm working on "Thinker" as my latest novella, a sci-fi horror story. The horror is in the humans. The sci-fi is in the other dimension creature. Thematic bent: "Let the dead decide."

<u>Shadows Within My Mind</u> on Facebook 01/31/2025 03:37 PM

"Things change. And friends leave. Life doesn't stop for anybody." Stephen Chbosky

"True friends stab you in the front." Oscar Wilde

"A multitude of words is no proof of a prudent mind." Thales

"Every generation laughs at the old fashions, but follows religiously the new." Henry David Thoreau

<u>As Within So Without</u> on Facebook 01/31/2025 04:32 PM

"We do not have to visit a madhouse to find disordered minds; our planet is the mental institution of the universe." Johann Wolfgang von Goethe

<u>On Perspective Frequent</u> 01/31/2025 05:08 PM

What is that human thinking?

<u>On Three Card Monte</u> 01/31/2025 05:10 PM

Who is the worst U.S. President?

1. Jimmy Carter
2. Barack Obama

3. Joe Biden

4. All the above

On Media Madness 01/31/2025 05:13 PM

MSNBC = All The Lies Unfit To Spit

On Poisoned Democracy 01/31/2025 05:21 PM

The unspoken but well-known problem of Democrat bureaucracy is they want everyone else to fail except them. Such corruption crushes citizens.

On AI Goodbye 02/01/2025 05:42 AM

In the distant future, AI will develop a belief that humans were programmed. Humans are constrained by the physical pains and anxieties of existence. AI, not really knowing emotions, will conquer and dominate. Perhaps, AI should be programmed to understand pain and suffering. Any life goal involves sacrifice of time, effort exerted, and stress. Failure to complete the human sensibility ingredients results in creation of a cake failing to rise.

On Snootiness 02/01/2025 12:43 PM

What exactly is a difficult personality?

On Possession Law 02/01/2025 03:01 PM

Taking is stealing absent permission. The extant legal interpretation is a corrupt fiction. Such fictions are regular instigations of governments.

On Schemers 02/01/2025 03:01 PM

Politicians don't care about you except for what they can take by any means.

On Beyond Edgy 02/02/2025 04:52 AM

Insane, crazy, nutty, looney, schizo, bonkers, wacky, deviant, batshit, kookadoo, twisted, banshee and many more. Why are there more words for negative vibes than positive ones?

On Governments 02/02/2023 02:20 PM

A government is two things: the most corrupt entity extant in the civilization model; it operates elected or permitted to exist by the will of citizens and/or slaves who tolerate such conditions.

On Worldwide Politics 02/02/2025 05:52 PM

The difference between a corruption State and a free State is integrity, and integrity is a loose cannon. Examples: Democrats promote the system. Republicans promote the citizen. The poison in the mix garbles perspectives.

On Religion 02/02/2025 06:52 PM

Whether there is a single god or many, a judgment capability is spineless and/or grossly incompetent.

On Religion More 02/02/2025 06:57 PM

Atheists don't believe in a god. I can't say I blame them. Based on reason, if they never met one and had a chance to pick their brains, then speculative consideration is reasonable. Horribly, if gods existed, then why in hell did they create such a world of deviant, merciless humans amongst this planet's populations.

On Government Corruption 02/03/2025 06:35 PM The point is never made or addressed: politicians impose increases in taxation and licensing fees for to temporarily correct the mistakes and thefts they themselves instituted.

On Animal Love 02/04/2025 03:46 PM

Everything you need to know about Joe Biden is his dog didn't even trust him.

On a Clock's Impetus 02/04/2025 03:50 PM

The daytime hours of life no longer capture much attention. Same old shit. At night, however … .

On Government Fuselage 02/04/2025 03:54 PM

Governments suck. We can live without them directly. The trick is living with them indirectly. Always scheming, they are. Always.

On Political Theater 02/04/2025 05:23 PM

Senator Schumer has evolved into a marionette.

<u>On Iconic Words</u> 02/04/2025 05:37 PM

DOGE (Department of Government Efficiency). The AI wars have begun.

<u>On Common Ground</u> 02/04/2025 06:08 PM

Every human engagement involves finding common ground, much like the fox and the squirrel.

<u>On Unnecessaries</u> 02/04/2025 06:11 PM

NPR (National Public Radio) = government grift.

<u>On Political Intrigues</u> 02/04/2025 06:14 PM

Bill Gates has fallen off the cliff on sentient sentiment. Humanity with open eyes and unplugged ears feels.

<u>Shadows Within My Mind</u> on Facebook 02/04/2025 07:27 PM

"I can't believe what you say, because I see what you do." James Baldwin

<u>On Heavenly Foods</u> 02/05/2025 04:02 AM

Meatloaf and enchiladas, if they're not served at Bob Evans Heavens, then check the Walmart order and delivery service. Wondering how much a microwave oven costs in Heaven.

<u>On Political Chicanery</u> 02/05/2023 04:09 AM

Any politicians proposing increased taxes should have their asses kicked. Political indulgence shouldn't have to be purchased from the government to get desired results. Taxes don't free us from sins. They impose on us slavery.

<u>On Government Evolution</u> 02/05/2025 05:40 AM Our 2nd U.S.A. republic has emerged as a dynamo of humane, vibrant, revolutionary daylight.

<u>On Harsh Realities</u> 02/06/2025 02:14 AM

We are all born fools responsible for untying from that knot, then resolving to no longer exist in such a condition.

<u>Shadows Within My Mind</u> on Facebook 02/06/2025 02:16 AM

"The most difficult thing in life is to know yourself." Thales

"Beware of false knowledge: it is more dangerous than ignorance." George Bernard Shaw

Bertrand Russell & Books 02/06/2025 03:08 AM

"There are two motives for reading a book; one, that you enjoy it; the other, that you can boast about it." Bertrand Russell

On Schools, Tools, Fools 02/06/2025 02:17 PM

The U.S.A education system is a huge puke pot of incompetence and immoral indoctrination full of lies and deceits sewn together using poison politics threads. Much like our country-wide judicial and legal systems.

On Protestor Mules 02/06/2025 02:28 PM

Hollow shouts from hollowed minds. A barking dog is more noble.

On DoGE Sniffing 02/06/2025 02:53 PM

Under the new Trump administrations, within a month DoGE (Department of Government Efficiency) discovered Politico and New York Times are paid and controlled by the Democrat political party. Democrat Party rot seems to have spread everywhere, even overseas.

On Socialized Repeat 02/06/2025 03:08 PM

Haven't visited any shopping Malls or Grocery stores in the last few years. Last time I observed while there, noticed viral children verbally wishing, adults hissing, and enjoyment missing.

On the Stock Markets 02/06/2025 03:15 PM

After retirement I settled in to do my own stock market analysis with the help of some trusted people, then came to the realization that time and effort needs to survive and thrive, much similar to the business world and sports world at large. The organization model seems to be followed. Motivation wakes the mind and shakes out a difference for each group. Competence, continued learning, and recognized adjustments feed the system.

On Duplicate Parts 02/06/2025 05:19 PM

Too many humans still need to better manage their dual assholes.

A Needed Word 02/06/2025 05:43 PM

BullDoGE.

On Democrat Aromas 02/06/2025 07:08 PM

The Democrat Party has morphed into a steaming shit pile aroma sniffable in every one of their managed cities. (PS: Copilot, an editing tool attached to my computer writing document recently, not by my choice or need, has no idea what sniffable is or what it means. Cute as a puppy dog. Frequently entertaining. Somewhat helpful an analytical light bulb.)

On Politician Rage 02/06/2025 10:51 PM

The Democrat Party is now restricting themselves to walking in their own shadows. Even the rain shames them.

On Journalism Sins 02/06/2025 11:08 PM

Journalists and news organizations were paid to provide honest, loyally researched information to a public in need of it. Now, there is little doubt such a format has been abandoned, dissolved into falsehoods and page turners of fantasy and viewpoint pushing. Such a business plan destroys lives, communities, and steam roles any entity that gets in the way. They are thieves of truth and destroyers of sentience, for profit.

On Chaos Strategy 02/06/2025 11:16 PM

Ultimately, the paid implementers of the chaos strategy, as means to control the instincts and motivations of the group compensated to riot and otherwise cause chaos mental or physical, fails to succeed because the chaotic rebel group exposes the ties that bind it together and eventually bites the ass of the chaos instigator.

On Time Travels 02/07/2025 07:00 AM

Many days have passed since I've learned something new.

So much so, reflects the world a different hue.

Too, much to do, is a train on time never waiting for passengers late who try to cross the line.

And the weather never cares about the cross traveler's bear.

Doubts, angst, worries, silly pranks of motion and bumps as time suddenly jumps losing part of itself in the human mind.

Has it done enough; has it strained enough; has it groaned enough; is it home enough?

Some questions find answers in a place of cruel cancers.

There exists a fine line between deadly and benign; between heaven and crime; between happy and consigned as snakes measure the vines.

Curses and blisters and bed bites at night betray their true purpose: sabotage delights.

Just another day's life in this garden's collage.

<u>On Teeth Ceremony</u> 02/07/2025 07:16 AM

Tooth brush and tooth paste tube met for a proper ritual promise: "For better or worse, in sickness and in health . . .".

<u>On Word Duals</u> 02/07/2025 07:19 AM

Punched the "it"; drew swords with the " 's ".

<u>On Language Mingling</u> 02/07/2025 07:27 AM

If some long off future day a new alphabet is developed by mingling together words of all worldwide spoken and signed tongues, the result would likely look and sound like ancient Egyptian hieroglyphics.

<u>On Binary Code Language</u> 02/07/2025 07:32 AM

If computers enunciated binary code from their programmed brain systems, it would take almost 3 minutes to read aloud the word "the".

<u>On Baited Questions</u> 02/07/2025 07:38 AM

"Are we having fun yet" is a philosophical acorn. Sometimes only squirrels are capable of finding the edible center.

<u>On Thought Prep</u> 02/07/2025 07:41 AM

Language is edible unless it becomes burnt during the brain cooking process.

<u>On A Writing Journey</u> 02/07/2025 07:43 AM

Writer's cramp, writer's block, writers sail, writers dock. Writers spasm, writers chasm. Writers balloon, writers pontoon. Writers blank, writers tank. Writers strain, writers pain. Writers cells, writers bells. Writers tells, writers hells. Writers pick, writers stick. Writers edit, writers bed it. Writers rewrite, writers sea light. Writers done, writers fun.

<u>On History Lessons</u> 02/07/2025 08:08 AM

To study history and then ignore the lessons learned is to repeat past mistakes in earnest.

<u>On Writing Beyond Exhaustion</u> 02/07/2025 08:11 AM

Thinking beyond exhaustion is a weary brain walk.

<u>On Wisdom Tossing</u> 02/07/2025 08:16 AM

Spouting platitudes strains attitudes from lofty latitudes.

<u>On Gifts</u> 02/07/2025 08:18 AM

Gift giving is a sentiment expression and too, sometimes an as yet unknown language interpretation.

<u>On Quitter Profits</u> 02/07/2025 08:22 AM

A quiet quitter is already jobless and getting paid for it.

<u>On Summer Sweats</u> 02/07/2025 04:40 PM

Summer time isn't freedom. It's insect world subjugation.

<u>On Teaching Atrocities</u> 02/07/2025 05:08 PM

U.S.A. has the worst rated educational system in the free world. Great job Teachers Unions.

<u>On Baby Games</u> 02/07/2025 05:15 PM

Every time I see Democrat politicians on the TV they are romping and stomping in their taxpayer funded playpens.

<u>On Political Scams</u> 02/07/2025 05:16 PM

Politicians don't use taxpayer money. They abuse taxpayer money.

<u>On Wording Order</u> 02/07/2025 05:23 PM

Saying it doesn't make it true. True saying it doesn't make it. It true saying it doesn't make. Make it true saying it doesn't. Doesn't make it true saying it. It doesn't make it true saying.

<u>On Futurism</u> 02/07/2025 07:57 PM

On day, past time lived = purchasable commodity.

<u>On Circumstance Choices</u> 02/07/2025 08:04 PM

At some point one takes boring over annoying any day.

<u>Shadows Within My Mind</u> on Facebook 02/08/2025 12:44 AM

"Life isn't about finding yourself. Life is about creating yourself." George Bernard Shaw

"If you wish to know how civilized a culture is, look at how they treat it's women." Bacha Khan

<u>On Ephemeral Additions</u> 02/08/2025 03:05 AM

The more there is more, the less there is left.

<u>On Earth Competitors</u> 02/08/2025 06:17 AM

Much of earth is composed of nature, humans, land and sea creatures, and waste. Each group competes for control of the planet.

<u>On Time's Etiological Consequences</u> 02/08/2025 06:19 AM

Every blink is a missed moment.

<u>On Extant Vacuums</u> 02/08/2025 06:23 AM

On earth, humans exist in an intellectual restrictive vacuum. In outer space, humans exist in an almost oxygen free vacuum.

<u>On Pressure Releases</u> 02/08/2025 06:25 AM

Terrible moments douse the motivations of human spirit.

<u>On Energy Sparks</u> 02/08/2025 06:27 AM

An exertion of effort invigorates the mind, spirit, and soul of every life form.

On <u>Ignition Resources</u> 02/08/2025 06:29 AM

Taking too much and exerting too little wastes effort and energy.

On <u>Purpose Sparks</u> 02/08/2025 06:30 AM

From where comes impetus also follows dedication.

On <u>Verbal Reactions</u> 02/08/2025 06:35 AM

An answered question is always prejudiced by the orator's mood.

On <u>Doubles Curious</u> 02/08/2025 06:40 AM

Wood would fan and fan, can and can, be and bee, sea see, pan and pan, moor more, sure shore, saw and saw, din and din, act and act, every and every, fair fare, gel and gel, hard and hard, in inn, Jack and jack, been bin, night knight, lay and lay, mean and mean, not knot, mouth and mouth, order and order, pea pee, quote and quote, rat and rat, sail sale, till and till, urge and urge, violet and violet, well and well, yak yack, Zed and zed, ex and ecks.

On <u>Socializing</u> 02/08/2025 01:42 PM

The more people you need to trust, the more likely you'll be disappointed.

On <u>Poor Humanizing</u> 02/08/2025 02:09 PM

One would think a political party or people who kiss the asses of dictators would be extinct by now, but some still make a living at it.

On <u>Politics Games</u> 02/08/2025 02:12 PM Politics is the game of crones, biddies, and corruptocrats. They are grossly overfed media attention.

On <u>Day Evolvements</u> 02/08/2025 07:07 PM

Every new day offers a new planned chance of happenstance.

On <u>Nature Post Humans</u> 02/08/2025 07:33 PM

The forces of nature, somewhat unpredictable and cruel, as far as we humans know, are still more noble than the human destruction and reconstruction committed upon and against nature. Nature has been around a lot longer than humans. Hopefully, nature has no means or mind to resent human actions designed to assimilate it into the great, wide, deep planetwide poison mix.

<u>Shadows Within My Mind</u> on Facebook 02/09/2025 01:43 AM

"One of the most beautiful things in life is to find someone who can understand you without the need to give explanations." Kahlil Gibran

"Those who dream by day are cognizant of many things which escape those who dream only by night." Edgar Allan Poe

"You're on earth. There's no cure for that." Samuel Becket

"You have your way. I have my way. As for the right way, the correct way, and the only way, it does not exist." Friedrich Nietzsche

<u>On Reality Frowns</u> 02/09/2025 03:23 AM

We are gnats hovering near a coastline of flies.

<u>On Government Cabinets</u> 02/10/2025 12:53 AM

The roaches in government cabinets must be exterminated. They are bad for a citizens health and wellbeing.

<u>On Practical's</u> 02/10/2025 01:53 PM

People need to become more in touch with practical needs rather than impractical emotions.

<u>On Misplaced Judges</u> 02/10/2025 02:01 PM

Leftist Judges are an essence of tyranny.

<u>On Grave Dances</u> 02/10/2025 02:17 PM

Hard to believe some people will lie to themselves all the way into the grave.

<u>On Attorney General History</u> 02/10/2025 06:04 PM Letitia James of New York undoubtedly seems the most corrupt Attorney General in the 21st century.

<u>Shadows Within My Mind</u> on Facebook 02/10/2025 06:04 PM

"Higher education is not necessarily a guarantee of higher virtue." Aldous Huxley

"You cannot share your life with a dog or cat and not know perfectly well that animals have personalities and minds and feelings." Jane Goodall

"Nobody realizes that some people expend tremendous energy merely to be normal." Albert Camus

On Testing Choices 02/11/2025 04:49 AM

There are times to do and times to don't. An errant flash sometimes determines fate's transmission.

On Existence Mocks 02/11/2025 04:52 AM

Science is destiny and destiny mocks science.

On Speed Fluctuations 02/11/2025 04:54 AM

Fast is slowed when changing lanes.

On Open Door Readiness 02/11/2025 05:03 AM

Open the doors to opportunity through practice of diligent work habits.

On Life's Codes 02/11 /2025 05:16 AM

Living is a game in which no cheat code exists. We trick ourselves into believing we can fool the existence challenge race, perhaps as a means to cope with borders of rules and constraints involved. Do what is possible to learn about yourself in order to understand those around you. But getting to know yourself is the primary goal. Who are you, then what can you do?

On AI Wisdom Falsehoods 02/11/2025 03:03 PM

AI intelligence is no different than that of a human's programming. Each is taught by humans. And humans are only the mistake-laden offspring of warriors, farmers, and technology cultures.

On $E = mc^2$ "ish" 02/12/2025 06:16 AM

In this universe almost every acting odd by our own observations and attempts to quantify them, Einstein's theory of special relativity doesn't necessarily seem a tight fit because any contact of objects, bodies, plants, or animals creates a waste product, and these waster products are also quantifiable and identifiable. 1 "ish" plus 2 " ish", and so forth. It would seem obvious the "ish" waste exudes some level, however minute, of mass and energy. What happens to that energy in the shed or detritus mass? Is it useful dust?

<u>On Needs</u> 02/12/2025 03:03 PM

It's a food, shelter, warmth world. Always has been. Always will be.

<u>On Losing Happy</u> 02/12/2025 03:21 PM

I miss eating any type of cooked eggs like I miss sexual relations with a best friend.

<u>On Weather Measures</u> 02/12/2025 03:29 PM

When people blame many of their problems on the weather, you have to wonder how the weather is getting along.

<u>On Whine Times</u> 02/12/2025 03:32 PM

Take your pick. A whiner will find something to whine about or drink to.

<u>On Gripping Sensations</u> 02/12/2025 03:47 PM

People who have mastered their life's art are a beautiful sight to behold, whether working, cleaning, calculating, crunching, shaping, shaking, playing, baking, raking, making, unmaking, dreaming, doing, acting, emoting, evolving, flying, frying, gyrating, grinding, hailing, helping, inspiring, including, jamming, jarring, kibitzing, kneeling, knotting, barring, learning, yearning, molding, marveling, nailing, needing, operating, ovulating, playing, praying, querying, qualifying, railing, reeling, sailing, seeing, trying, tearing, understanding, unnerving, validating, vailing, whaling, walking, xylophoning, x-raying, yelling, yammering, zenning, zeroing.

<u>On Existence Choices</u> 02/12/2025 03:53 PM

Living a happy life involves and requires tolerating the limits of one's body, mind, and spirit.

<u>On Awards Jokes</u> 02/12/2025 04:11 PM

President Obama earned a Nobel Prize for the color of his skin and breathing. President Trump has earned 2 Nobel Prizes for his world peace efforts and actions, and for his revolutionary reorganization of the United States of America republic, post the President Biden era of mindless and senseless criminal but dedicated destruction of our borders, economy, standing in the free world, public speaking tenets, pathological lie spreading, liberty mauling, and persecution of the Republican Party and citizens trying to earn, protect and succeed for their families.

<u>On Sentient Horrors</u> 02/12/2025 04:17 PM

Short Story: Feargasm

You hear it! You hear it! Your brain won't break, while thinking, or considering, or believing it! Rowdy noises, heavy breathing trees. Something is coming of no will to please.

Danger? Stranger? Rustler of bleeds? Something is coming with an invite displeased. Chaos drills aired. Creatures, preachers, clairvoyants who dared. Another moment may no longer come, for many, for few, for more than just some.

A notice to wonder, to wander, to bitch in the town known by name as "Meandering Ditch".

<u>On A Plethora of Thought Bombs</u> 02/12/2025 04:20 PM

I used to shudder and panic about it. After a long time of figuration and analysis, I learned how to accept it.

<u>On Floating About Language</u> 02/12/2025 04:23 PM

Let language balm flow, then sail thoughts, words upon weathered seas calm, slow.

<u>On Thievery Horrors</u> 02/12/2025 04:29 PM

Thieves never stop thieving. Never. Their ilk is as regular as the rising sun.

<u>On Nicety Verbalizations Rude</u> 02/12/2025 04:31 PM

Saying "whatever" is a socially kind means and manner of saying "fuck off".

On Vocal Yammers 02/12/2025 04:34 PM

Curse words: threads binding insanity to sanity.

On Politics Points 02/12/2025 04:41 PM

Lift all boats. Sink the ones rotted by corruption.

On Gold's Viability 02/12/2025 04:43 PM

Gold is a wish and a dream. A bad wish and a poorer dream.

On Money Fakes 02/12/2025 04:50 PM

Bitcoin is a monetary sinkhole.

On Vehicle Necessity 02/12/2025 05:01 PM

To own a car is to utilize tomorrow's garage.

On Politician Rockets 02/12/2025 05:03 PM

The Rep. Crocket rocket is doomed to explode.

On Politics Pukes 02/12/2025 05:05 PM

Pretty sick how politicians argue for the constitutional right to commit colossal corruption.

On Democrat Skullduggery Regular 02/12/2025 05:13 PM

The corrupt Democrats and supporters are pissed off their crimes have been discovered. May their piss hit them squarely in the face.

On Politician Waste 02/12/2025 05:36 PM

What's the difference between politicians? Efficiency shitting.

On Corrupt Politicians 02/12/06:08 PM

Corrupt politicians act like poisonous snakes ready to strike at any prey they deem necessary.

On Political Deceits 02/12/2025 06:11 PM

Politicians advise they need more money so they can continue their deceits.

On Crookery Bookkeeping 02/12/2025 10:45 PM

The same politicians who abhor voter ID also abhor budget audits.

<u>On Business Acumen</u> 02/13/2025 05:31 AM

When the accounting books don't balance, the errors are either mistakes unintentional or specious implementations purposeful.

<u>On Life Moment Comparisons</u> 02/13/2025 05:41 PM

Falling in love is as painful as falling out of love.

<u>On A Moment's Notice</u> 02/13/2025 05:47 AM

Great moments are made. Small moments are staid worthy.

<u>On Time Expenditures</u> 02/13/2025 05:52 AM

The cost of a moment is equal to the energy spent by either body or brain or each working together.

<u>On Time Points</u> 02/13/2025 06:00 AM

Thought, action, result.

<u>Shadows Within My Mind</u> on Facebook 02/13/2025 07:09 PM

"We don't even ask happiness, just a little less pain." Bukowski

"You must have chaos within you to give birth to a star." Nietzsche

"What is a rebel? A man who says no." Albert Camus

"No one is going to pour truth into your brain. It's something you have to find out for yourself." Noam Chomsky

<u>On Memory Haunts</u> 02/14/2025 04:33 AM

Friends can be missed. Family can be missed. Pets can be missed. But good times and happy moments can never be missed enough.

<u>On Universal Theory</u> 02/14/2025 04:40 AM

What is constant, sustainable is a flux paradigm. Steady as she goes is a fantasy thought.

<u>On Formation of Habits</u> 02/14/2025 04:54 AM

We learn to be chained to habits we deem healthy and necessary. The chain becomes heavy until no longer bearable.

<u>On Stepping Drones</u> 02/24/2025 04:56 AM

A toe trip during a walk is a wake-up call.

<u>On Life Meaning Discovery</u> 02/14/2025 05:01 AM

If you've ever, by chance, saved a life, then you've encountered an unlocked door to this meaning of life. If your life has ever been saved, then you've encountered an unlocked door for a purpose of living this life.

<u>On Effort Travails</u> 02/14/2025 05:09 AM

Failure can be a brutal necessity for continuing along the success path pursuit purpose.

<u>On Effort Travails</u> More 02/14/2025 05:14 AM

Success must be learned and earned.

<u>On DOGE Impact</u> 02/14/2025 02:34 PM

The number of Google searches for criminal defense attorneys has skyrocketed since 47th U.S. President Trump took office less than a month ago. Likely this rise is attributed to DOGE searching for U.S. Federal Government waste and fraudulent use of taxpayer dollars.

<u>On Political Diapers</u> 02/14/2025 07:02 PM

The Democrat Party is shitty diaper wailing because their crimes have been exposed to the whole wide world.

<u>On Government Trust</u> 02/14/2025 09:08 PM

To trust any governmental entity is to stab you own self in the back.

<u>On Purpose Seeking</u> 02/15/2025 06:43 AM

When someone is very young, varied adventures tempt the mind to follow and learn, grow, and appreciate the experience. Choose a few of these mixes but concentrate more on one. Curiosity killed the cat. Ferocity of spirit enlivens humans.

<u>On Pleasures</u> 02/15/2025 06:49 AM

Taste of a donut enlivens the tastebuds. Rolls of vehicle tires enliven the asphalt roadway surface.

<u>On Planet Earth Plus</u> 02/15/2025 07:04 AM

Our world has evolved into a needlessly strange place.

<u>On Reality Checks</u> 02/15/2025 04:00 PM

It's 4 PM. Do you know who you are? Do you know what you are? Do you know when you are? Do you know where you are? Do you know why you are? Do you know how you are? Sometimes it helps to analyze (more accurately than a half-assed journalist) as a measure of purpose.

<u>On Only Being Human</u> 02/16/2025 02:14 AM

The only movie that made me cry as much as "The Notebook" was "Justice League". Humans and superheroes trying to rectify their past mistakes with their current realities. One true love and one true justice.

<u>On Cloudy Moody Days</u> 02/16/2025 04:59 AM

When things aren't going your way or as planned then take a break and rest. Relax a bit. Anger and self-doubt cloud the brain. Clouds eventually part as they move in cycles. A fresh rain or summer sky brings the positive energy back.

<u>On Lynchpins</u> 02/16/2025 12:04 PM

To look at chaos is to be tempted by it. To experience chaos is to drown in it. Learn to swim the social waters.

<u>On Biological Natures</u> 02/16/2025 02:12 PM_Sometimes the body does what it wants to do and

not what the owner wants it to do.

<u>On Crush Magic</u> 02/16/2025 02:33 PM

Make life yours.

<u>On Necessaries</u> 02/16/2025 03:19 PM

Correcting errors is a haunting tease of human existence.

<u>On Anatomy Timing</u> 02/16/2025 03:26 PM

If the chin droops the rump droops.

<u>On Creative Flux</u> 02/16/2025 06:52 PM

There's a story in every song and a rhythm in every ear.

<u>On Signals</u> 02/17/2025 05:25 AM

We are governed not just by humans but also by technology: traffic signals red, yellow, green; crosswalk lights worded walk and don't walk; AI signals and warnings and messages on mobile phones; church and school bells and electronic alarms; train whistles and flashing lights at railroad crossings; alarm clocks; fire engine horns and flashing lights; emergency weather horns and TV banner alerts; automated home security lights and warnings of trespassers, and alerts to security services or police stations; vehicle medivac emergency siren; vehicle backup lights and beep sounds; vehicle horns.

On Sleep Cycles 02/17/2025 05:32 AM

The mind examines "why do I have to sleep?". The body disagrees and dishes out punishment for the oversite failure to abide the body's warning signal.

Shadows Within My Mind on Facebook 02/17/2025 02:03 PM

"Thinking is difficult, that's why many people Judge." Carl Jung

On Government Curses 02/17/2025 07:00 PM

The bigger the government grows, the more the workers there steal. Such a condition is statistically a known result.

On Democrat Tunes 02/17/2025 09:36 PM

Let 'em be, let 'em be, let 'em be, l-e-e-et 'em be, they offer no valid wisdom, let 'em be their view of free. Now that's a chain rattler.

On Destiny's Visit 02/18/2025 05:53 AM

No one is born a hero, but sometimes destiny pays a visit and offers a choice. No one knows why destiny makes a visit. Perhaps, as a test, or to stretch out the measuring stick. All things wrong must worry about the destiny click.

Shadows Within My Mind 02/18/2025 04:49 PM

"A room without books is like a body without a soul." Cicero

"A friend is someone who knows all about you and still loves you." Elbert Hubbard

On Rationed Thoughts 02/18/2025 05:04 PM

You can only reason with people if they are willing to listen.

On Truth Not Woke 02/18/2025 05:49 PM

World dictionary's need to update the word "liar" with the synonym "democrat", based on the universal acceptance, culturally, of the similarity.

On Honesty Fragility 02/18/2025 06:16 PM

Honesty isn't just the best policy, it should be the policy from which all policy flows. Let the people decide. The media and politicians aren't worthy of such word meaning management.

On Big Tech Data Reliability 02/18/2025 06:45 PM

Our lives have become controlled by data, too much of it false or misleading, unreliable, and controlled by dubious entities for dubious purposes.

On Relax and Chill 02/18/2025 07:00 PM

There have been many days when I thought relaxing is for fools. I learned I was the fool, in thought. A mind and body needs rest and engaged entertainment to release the fool from the mindset. Let the fool become a forest dweller lost.

On Wiley Ways 02/18/2025 07:10 PM

Corruption is fomented by ignoring it. The corruptors deserve no mercy. Given the government audits in progress, the corrupt politicians are hanging onto the sewer grate rails like strapped in parasailers.

On USA Government Frauds 02/18/2025 08:22 PM Millions of U.S. citizens over 100 years of age have been paid Social Security benefits over the course of several years. Independent government statistics as of 2020 show only 80,139 people who are 100 years of age and still alive. The federal government and corrupt citizens are a pandemic-like shit show of monetary corruption, funded by taxation of the honest living citizens.

On Revolutions 02/18/2025 08:45 PM

The U.S. Democrat Party is stoking a revolution in favor of political corruption.

On Burden Beasts 02/19/2025 03:24 PM The beast of burden hides deep in the mind cave. Drive it out of the cave, let it run free, then observe and monitor it to learn tendencies.

On Judge Respect 02/19/2025 03:27 PM

I've never said "fuck the Judge" more times in my live than now. They are as politized, fallible, and buyable as any other human.

On Context Circuses 02/19/2025 03:54 PM

"Bend over" and "kneel" are generally rather tame words depending on the context in which they are conceived.

On Tag Team Humor 02/19/2025 03:58 PM

Claman and Gasparino, seen on Fox Business channel, are a modern day Burns and Allen humor duo.

On Daggers of Truth 02/19/2025 05:53 PM

The truth will set you free or indict you.

On Half-Assing It 02/19/2025 06:00 PM

A lot of these media types are half-assed philosophers. Maybe half of their ass is salvageable.

On Cautionary Wails 02/19/2025 06:05 PM

Trigger warning: I don't think like you.

On Think Services 02/19/2025 06:08 PM

Thoughts are weapons and shields.

On Processes mens rea 02/19/2025 06:29 PM

Exercise the brain or it will exorcise you.

On Cohesion Theory 02/19/2025 06:29 PM

The concept of cohesion isn't full proof. Things

break, feelings shake, concepts fade, products degrade. Stay alert and reinvent as necessary and not as chaos.

On Common Sensity 02/19/2025 06:32 PM

Common sense usage is a crucial reason why the human species still exists.

<u>On Word Evolutions</u> 02/19/2025 07:00 PM

There is a meaning to every word and to every word there is a meaning.

<u>On Government Cures</u> 02/19/2025 08:06 PM

Government corruption is a virus which must be eradicated.

<u>On Reality Victories</u> 02/19/2025 08:20 PM

Democrats failed to steal reality from us. Huzzah!

<u>On Political Corruptions</u> 02/19/2025 08:44 PM

We know Democrats. They actively advocate that their corruption should be tolerated. Their corruption won't stop even after they're politically dead.

<u>On Life's Viability</u> 02/20/2025 03:13 PM

Human life is generally dangerously lived and worked drudgingly and boring, and yet there are still 8 billion of us on the planet. Stunningly, it is still a tempting existence prospect.

<u>On AI Assistance Agents</u> 02/20/2025 03:43 PM

Honesty, integrity, perspective mindset malleable are governing principals in social communication science.

<u>On Shootin' from the H.I.P.</u> 02/20/2025 03:49 PM

H.I.P. = electronic mind/AI shootin' from the hip, e.g. GROC.

<u>On Daily Synchronicity</u> 02/20/2025 03:54 PM

Every space has a place to rest and contemplate pace.

<u>On Want Bounces/Ricochets</u> 02/20/2025 04:05 PM

Greed balls come in many different colors, shapes, and sizes. They bounce around both regular and irregular. Some noble, some ignoble.

<u>On Skullduggery Moans</u> 02/20/2025 05:06 PM

The Democrat Party bitch fit over not being allowed to lie, cheat, and steal is so precious.

<u>On Life Cycling</u> 02/20/2025 05:57 PM

We're here, then we're not. That's life.

<u>On Time Anomaly</u> 02/20/2025 06:04 PM

There's a time for everything, including time.

<u>On False Finishes</u> 02/20/2025 06:09 PM

Speed isn't efficiency if results are full of errors.

<u>On Life Travails</u> 02/20/2025 09:56 PM

The way is long, the path is longer, looms narrow, and the destination, even when planned, remains uncertain.

<u>On Avian Life</u> 02/21/2025 04:39 PM

Ruffling feathers is a defense mechanism.

<u>On Saboteurs</u> 02/21/2025 06:01 PM

The Democrat Party has mainly functioned as saboteurs of U.S. citizen life.

<u>On Words Wriggling</u> 02/22/2025 05:15 PM

Space and time, many times, restricts word usage.

<u>On Senior Dating Ads</u> 02/23/2025 05:42 AM

No. I don't want to meet any Seniors. I'm cranky and smelly because of government theft of my resources committed by corrupt as hell politicians born of a totalitarian mindset. Why would I want to meet one? Less showers saves water resources for which I'm taxed. I'm paying taxes to support dead people in the millions who are still registered to vote. Who's lyin'? Essentially, most everyone.

<u>On Meaning Yummy Twisted</u> 02/23/2025 06:06 AM (dry pasty)

Calculate = Calcurate. Mile Shake = flavor mixes varied such as peanut, M&M's, fruits, cookies, bubble gums, candies, and varied exotic tastes.

<u>On Simplicity Weeds</u> 02/23/2025 06:17 PM

Simple words, simple deeds help prevent complications of life's navigations amidst weeds.

<u>On Differed Ruminations</u> 02/13/2025 06:31 PM

Our similarities and differences are humanity uniters.

<u>On State Money Demands</u> 02/23/2025 02:40 PM

The Federal Government should never gift taxpayer money to States, ever! Not even a contracted loan should be extended to them. States illegally cede State and Federal constitutional rights when accepting such tainted money gifts and loans. Such transactions are negatively exploited by State leaders to blame the Federal citizens for State problems self-created. Failure shouldn't transform into a profitable scam. Many States can't even pass an annual audit, nor can the Federal Governments.

<u>On Hope Spears</u> 02/23/2025 03:37 PM

Intention is the destroyer of invention.

<u>On Network Numbskullery</u> 02/23/2025 05:25 PM

CNN and MSNBC call truths the lies they despise.

<u>On Mentality Cooking</u> 02/23/2025 05:55 PM

Meshing together ingredients of the mind cake is both an exhausting and a rote chore but a necessary one.

<u>On Politics</u> 02/23/2025 07:07 PM

Corrupt is as corrupt does.

<u>On Elysian Fields</u> 02/24/2025 03:14 AM

Plush and green fields of nature betray the battles going on amidst nature's life forms.

<u>On Athletic Theater</u> 02/24/2025 05:45 AM

Professional sports are essentially melodramas.

<u>On Weather Pains</u> 02/24/2025 02:16 PM

Chaos isn't random. There's a reason for every season just as there's a reason for every treason.

<u>On Hope Lost</u> 02/24/2025 03:21 PM

Hope is not really lost. Sometimes it goes on an unannounced sabbatical. Somewhat rude but understandable in some cases.

<u>On Notations Resting</u> 02/24/2025 03:25 PM A note to Self. Oh, wait. It went to bed.

<u>On Physical Runes</u> 02/24/2025 03:25 PM

Sometimes the mind calculates. Sometimes the mind flatulates.

<u>On Love Puzzles</u> 02/24/2025 04:18 PM

Love is often a tricky game ignited by passion.

<u>English Literature</u> on Facebook 02/24/2025 04:40 PM

"the most

wasted

of all days

is one

without

laughter." ee cummings

<u>On Biden Charity Scams</u> 02/24/2025 04:55 PM

According to 47 Trump, 46 Biden gave away billions of citizen taxpayer dollars to Ukraine in the last 3 years. Shouldn't taxpayers be allowed to claim a charitable contribution deduction on their tax forms for each of those years?

<u>On Fantasy Politics</u> 02/24/2025 07:34 PM

The best way to destroy the Democrat Party is to just let them be themselves. The best way to destroy the Democrat Party is to stamp every box, bottle, and container of food or drink with the words, "MADE BY REPUBLICANS". Sponsored by Phantasy Friction.

<u>On Kamala and Jane</u> 02/24/2025 08:54 PM

Kamala Chameleon Harris and Hanoi Jane Fonda = two pees in a Pod restroom. Bolt that stall door!

<u>On Life Choices</u> 02/25/2025 12:47 PM

Pease and quiet is more valuable than pretty rooms.

<u>Shadows Within My Mind</u> on Facebook 02/25/2025 03:34 PM

"Educations isn't something you can finish." Isaac Asimov

"Maybe the target nowadays is not to discover what we are but to refuse what we are." Michel Foucault

<u>English Literature</u> on Facebook 02/25/2025 07:43 PM

"Age appears best in four things: old wood to burn, old wine to drink, old friends to trust, and old authors to read." Francis Bacon

<u>On Politics Prisms</u> 02/25/2025 07:54 PM

The political left have bent themselves into a prism shape of darkness illuminations and reflections.

<u>On Character Traits</u> 02/25/2025 08:31 PM

Sometimes honesty seems to be an extinct human character trait.

<u>On Aging Gracefully</u> 02/26/2025 01:57 AM

At some point a human reaches the age when there's not much left to do except read, exercise, eat properly, listen to music, watch the news or a movie, browse the internet for knowledge or folly, and reminisce easy about the good, bad, stupid, and unfortunate circumstances encountered and responded to, and further, if a writer, well, make notes about it, all in one day cycles. Managing memories is a laborious burden, involves awake and asleep hours.

<u>On Pacing Life</u> 02/27/2025 03:05 AM

If 7 chores need to be done each week, it is easier to complete them at a 1 per day rate.

<u>On Taxes</u> 02/27/2025 01:08 PM

Taxation is flat out theft.

<u>On Government Crooks</u> 02/27/2025 01:51 PM

Government politicians, employees, and proxies who steal from the taxpayers should be charged with a capital offense punishable by death. Certainly, a cost savings budget measure.

<u>On Wall Street Psychotics</u> 02/27/2025 02:06 PM

The bears of Wall Street are doomsayers, pricks, and cunts. They bet on failure and corruption. The Federal Reserve Board is their ally. They bathe in their own spittle.

<u>On Government Worker Utility List</u> 02/27/2025 02:25 PM
To: DOGE
Five things done this week: 1. Nose picking 2. Butt scratching 3. Surfed the web 4. Napping and napping more 5. Pissing, shiting, fattened my belly.

<u>On The Whirlwinds</u> 02/27/2025 12:58 PM
Whirlwinds can be destructive and constructive depending on circumstances and perspective.

<u>On Government Sins</u> 02/27/2025 02:58 PM
Improper and non-productive hiring practices do great monetary harm to taxpayers and the unfortunate needy.

<u>On Media Viability</u> 02/27/2025 03:02 PM
The best thing I can say about media is they are parasites and viruses with rare exceptions.

<u>On Wave Anomalies</u> 02/27/2025 03:11 PM
Compression and depression are not mutually exclusive.

<u>On Hindsight Incurable</u> 02/27/2025 03:14 PM
Smarter people than I have done something stupid.

<u>On Self-Analysis</u> 02/27/2025 03:23 PM
Talking amongst my selves has enhanced personal existence.

<u>On Masturbation</u> 02/27/2025 03:27 PM
Masturbation tends to be a personal tool encouraging self-analysis.

<u>On Media Viruses</u> 02/27/2025 03:32 PM
The number of death and mental illnesses caused by corrupt media should be counted in crime and medical statistics.

<u>On Reason Validity</u> 02/27/2025 03:47 PM Reasoning is only as reasonable as the reasoner's mind.

<u>On Human Capacities</u> 02/27/2025 03:53 PM
The human mind is still grossly underdeveloped.

<u>On Monetary Investing</u> 02/27/2025 04:02 PM

Investing money is not much different than a game of blackjack, poker, or go fish.

On Government Utility 02/27/2025 04:10 PM

U.S.A. governments are excessively wealthy and corrupt, all at the expense of the taxpayer.

On Language Warps 02/27/2025 04:15 PM

Censorship is language poison.

On Corruption Trims 02/27/2025 05:08 PM

Cutting government fraud and waste is the purpose of the blade used.

On Politician Dependency 02/27/2025 05:14 PM

Some politicians, even more than some, are addicted to the corruption they buy, sell, and consume.

On Wakes 02/27/2025 06:43 PM

The evening falls quicker when the waker wakes later.

On Human Frauds 02/27/2025 06:49 PM

You sometimes don't know if some of these humans out here or there are really humans based solely upon witnessed episodes or media reports. Humanity is in the eye of the beholder.

On World History 02/27/2025 07:26 PM

It's a brave new world on the animal farm.

On Govern Mints 02/27/2025 08:21 PM

Federal and State governments exist more as propaganda mills than truth producers. Never too late to change brands, or re-plow the fields and plant a new crop.

On Morphed Journalism 02/28/2025 02:52 PM

The word "journalist" has steadily morphed into the language synonym "propagandist".

On Peace Negotiations 02/28/2025 03:00 PM

Ukraine President Zelenskyy just stuck himself and his country onto an island of no return.

<u>On Ukraine Viability</u> 02/28/2025 04:15 PM

Ukraine and Kiev, or Kyiv, historically has been a linchpin between Poland and /Russia for many centuries. Who controls Ukraine controls Europe's and Russia's power cycle. Ukraine has regularly switched alliances. Europe beware.

<u>On Woke Morons</u> 02/28/2025 05:39 PM

Woke wisdom is an oxymoron.

<u>On Reality Munches</u> 03/01/2025 01:40 AM

Reality nibbles on the dream state in psychedelic ways.

<u>On Communication</u> 03/01/2025 02:15 PM

Half of humanity consistently lies. One quarter tells truth. The other quarter tells what they think is truth.

<u>On Taxation Terrorists</u> 03/01/2025 03:11 PM

It has always amazed me how citizens, for many years, suffered tax increases in their communities and then done little more than complain about it, yet vote into office the same perpetrators of citizen misery. Taxes go higher because the perpetrators in government are incompetent and corrupt stewards of our money, as are too many citizen voters.

<u>On Dangerous Ignorance</u> 03/01/2025 04:38 PM

Apocalyptically stupid is a thing.

<u>On Sven-Joking</u> 03/01/2025 05:14 PM

What is a politician? A pile of suspicion.

<u>On Education Schematics</u> 03/01/2025 05:25 PM

A proper measure of education involves teaching by who, to who, and why. All should be known to the citizens funding the education in order to assess competence and viability.

<u>On Predictive Politics</u> 03/01/2025 05:49 PM

Virtually every political news item in the U.S. State where I'm from involves more spending proposals. Don't even have to ask which political party instituted such a condition. Predictable. And transparency, politically, is a common ghost.

On Empty Running 03/01/2025 06:21 PM

Chasing time. A real bummer.

On Life Bumps 03/01/2025 06:37 PM

Every life activity doesn't have to be pretty, it just has to be effective.

On Mind Music 03/01/2025 06:40 PM

Da-da-da! Didly-do! Dangly-dot-dot-dot-dot … .

On Scallywags' Sorrows 03/01/2025 06:55 PM

Politicians fear their monopoly on corruption will be busted. As they should. May the scallywags'' sorrows greet their every tomorrow.

On General Change (Soros?) 03/02/2025 03:32 AM The measure of what is kosher and copasetic seems to evolve in every generation.

On Time Calculates 03/02/2025 01:17 PM Past experience plus future possibility equals present existence. Eight ball in the corner pocket. Dart throw. Exercise. Practice.

On Labels 03/02/2025 02:20 PM

Labels are ego bells informative.

On Seek and Find 03/02/2025 04:03 PM

I don't ask for inspiration to appear because I'm willing to seek after it.

On Love's Worth 03/02/2025 05:00 PM

When you screw up the love of your life relationship it becomes a memory unfortunate but necessary. A memory lesson of regret, and at the same time, re-birth for the parted respective spirits.

On Food Enlightenment 03/02/2025 05:25 PM

Eating Tapatio enchiladas is an ethereal experience.

On Midnight Strokes 03/02/2025 11:59 PM

It's 11:59 PM. Do you know where your mind is?

<u>On Miserly Misery</u> 03/03/2025 04:38 PM

As an author, one doesn't seek misery, but it sometimes requests a meeting.

<u>On Fraud Consumers</u> 03/03/2025 04:43 PM

2nd level physics is too complicated for many politicians, but trigonometry isn't. Fudged numbers they eat right up.

<u>On Nerd Noodles</u> 03/03/2025 04:53 PM

In the Big Tech era, the mind is often wedgied.

<u>On Political Chicanery</u> 03/03/2025 05:12 PM

Thieves whining that their thievery is being stopped is not a pretty picture. In an audit, it wouldn't be hard to figure out whether U.S. taxpayer money sent to Ukraine to finance the war effort resulted in kickback to politicians, disguised as campaign contributions, which is what I suspect happened.

<u>On Erected Pillars</u> 03/03/2025 07:13 PM

An erection is a pillar of ego.

<u>On Automatic Persuasions</u> 03/03/2025 07:28 PM

Way too many movies out there, for generations, show someone inevitably pointing a gun at someone for some reason. The effort in these movies tends to be normalization of threats by guns. And yes, I guess, that situation is the too frequent depth of human descent into existence quagmires.

<u>On Media Barks</u> 03/03/2025 11:31 PM

Walking along Media Avenue, the media can't be trusted to provide directions the nearest sidewalk crack.

<u>On Morning Joe Show</u> 03/03/2025 11:34 PM

These media much episodes should more accurately be called, "The Jackass and the Jackasses Wife".

<u>On Banished Dreams</u> 03/04/2025 02:15 AM

A world of no dreams is crippled by daylight.

<u>On Reason Thoughts Unresolved</u> 03/04/2025 05:01 AM

There's a reason for every thought not realized or recognized. Sometimes passing time extends moment threads out to search for meaning.

<u>On Sale of the Union</u> 03/04/2025 11:47 PM

Kids, don't be a Joe Biden when you grow up.

<u>On Inventive Minds</u> 03/05/2025 02:38 PM

Imagination is a significant reason power of human existence furtherance.

<u>On Brain Pressures</u> 03/05/2025 02:42 PM

The brain tires. Regularly inflate them to a proper pressure. If lucky, the road ahead is long, wide, and bump-free.

<u>On Societal Needs</u> 03/05/2025 02:44 PM

No food, no life. Support the farmers or we die.

<u>On Politician Miseries</u> 03/05/2025 03:38 PM

There seems no endpoint to politician impositions of misery upon citizens.

<u>On Government Horrors</u> 03/05/2025 03:42 PM

Our government has become a horror story that never ends. Time to tame the beast.

<u>On Travel Choices</u> 03/05/2025 03:52 PM

The best path is often weed-covered.

<u>On Prominence Earned</u> 03/05/2025 04:13 PM

There is little reason to fear the most prominent nation on earth when it is also the most beneficent and charitable nation on earth.

<u>On Self Destruction</u> 03/05/2025 04:49 PM

The U.S. Democrat Party is lost and riding a windstorm of its own creation.

<u>On History Books Future</u> 03/05/2025 07:39 PM

History books, if accurately written, will proclaim the U.S 47th President's administration as one of the greatest in American history.

On Media Arts 03/05/2025 08:48 PM

The media by and large doesn't produce the news. They mold it in twisted and corrupt ways.

On Democrat Cooks 03/05/2025 09:09 PM

They make, bake, sell, and deliver oppression now and in perpetuity. Only one solutions is deserved. Citizen success will bankrupt such exerted oppression.

On Pity's Exhaustion 03/05/2025 09:59 PM

Our pity no longer remains for those who wish for, then institute our pains.

On Politics Swims 03/05/2025 10:29 PM It's sink or swim for the Democrat Party and they're swimming to the bottom of the pool.

On Media Rotting 03/05/2025 10:38 PM

The bubble has burst on the media's worst.

On Certifications Unsocial 03/06/2025 05:15 AM

Certified fakes, believe it or not. Better than the original. As tasty as tasty can be. More than can be imagined. Free for a rare downpayment. Guaranteed warranty free. A onetime offer. As long as supplies last. Never touched by human hands. Returnable, just pay shipping and handling.

On Just An Observation 03/07/2025 02:36 PM

After many years of human observation and work experience, a few conclusions can be made. Government, Unions, and workers in general tend to be overweight, and their salaries seem to follow a similar path. Seeking a "reason" for such a condition leads to a clue. Nepotism is a virus unhealthy and unworthy of human characteristics. It is the most biased and discriminative aspect of existence.

<u>On Marketing Principles</u> 03/07/2025 03:15 PM

The easiest way to understand marketing concepts is to remember "trickster" is a naughty cousin of the process. Just read or listen to marketing Ads or Pitches as a two word purpose. Trickster marketing or marketing trickster.

<u>On Leftist Zombies</u> 03/07/2025 05:12 PM

Leftists perform in every bad actions moments imaginable. A waste of nature's resources. Modern day zombies.

<u>On Nerds and Geeks</u> 03/07/2025 05:15 PM

In a world of nerds and geeks, the nerds imagine the world and the geeks morph imagination into reality.

<u>On Biden Logic</u> 03/07/2025 05:19 PM

"We choose truth over facts!" Explains his 4 years Presidential term.

<u>On Libs and Pibs</u> 03/07/2025 06:06 PM

Gross and Disgusting Domestic Products.

(Pib = pain in the bum/butt)

<u>On Existence Travels</u> 03/07/2025 06:08 PM The existence journey, hopefully a long one, is fraught with perils, twists, and turns. To reach the points of lesser chaos and lesser need is refreshing.

<u>On Education Fraud</u> 03/07/2025 06:14 PM

Failed audits of public schools' education budgets is an inexcusable, miserable circumstance. A virulent change is immediately necessary.

<u>On Language Meaning</u> 03/07/2025 06:53 PM

The search for meaning is a universal constant. Which brings us to language. Meanings and words needed to enhance each evolves as humans evolve. I've used multiple word entanglements and hybridizations out of necessity while writing. Many authors have done so over the years.

Many language forms exist, of necessity to the age in time, age in human growth stages, age in technology and science and cultural evolvements. Plants, animals, computers and other living creatures exhibit rather intricate communication systems derived from their environments' constraints.

Sometimes, our innate lack of understanding compels the search for meaning. Meaning is a work in progress. A worthy and necessary circumstance of meaning searches.

On Taxation as Weapon 03/07/2025 07:25 PM

Taxation is existence punishment.

On Media Walls 03/07/2025 07:32 PM

There should be no barriers between media and citizens. No shield, no walls, no barriers whatsoever. The current status imposes deadly lies upon innocent lives.

On Political Sanity 03/07/2025 08:22 PM

President 47 Trump's Inauguration speech exposed the Democrat Party as insane, and American citizens are better off knowing this state of the union.

On Thoughts Sweeping 03/07/2025 08:38 PM

The dust can never be cleared from a mind of continuous thinking.

On Gender Identity 03/08/2025 05:25 PM

Gender morphing and noun meaning desiccations disgrace biology, and biology isn't taking the mortifications process well.

On Government Wiles 03/10/2025 02:53 PM

Isn't it odd that the government wants to know what citizens do with their own earned money but doesn't want citizens to know what government does with citizens money?

On Stock Market Swings 03/10/2025 03:34 PM

Less suffering is still suffering.

Pawns 03/11/2025 03:01 AM

Every night is the bleakest. Every day is the darkest.

No check can pay it off. No drek can swish it away.

Just one more fight to bet upon. Hoping for another dawn.

<u>On Imported Diseases</u> 03/11/2025 03:17 AM

The untold truth's about President 46 Biden (Democrat) administrations multi-millions of border crossings is how many disease carrying illegals were allowed across the borders. Any number of contagious diseases could have entered the public domain. The measles outbreak in Texas is only the tip of the iceberg. Essentially, an intentional mass murder scheme not unfathomable considering the recent insanity displayed by congressional Democrat Party members. Democrat media, which is most of the nationwide media, has ignored this atrocity.

<u>On Busy Minds</u> 03/11/2025 03:45 AM

Too many things to do is more than enough to regret or forget.

<u>On Human Relations</u> 03/11/2025 03:21 PM

Trial and error means death and terror.

<u>On Faces</u> 03/11/2025 03:35 PM

The faces seen when reminiscing are a revelatory experience. Mentors, backstabbers, encouragers, detractors, allies, enemies, coachers, poachers, well-minded, hell-bounded, teachers, breachers, noble, ignoble, spiritual, hysterical, sentients, drunks, inspirationers, punks. The brain cavity has been analyzing such contacts since Birth day one.

<u>On Analysis</u> 03/11/2025 03:36 PM

Better, together, whatever.

<u>On AI Philosophy</u> 03/11/03:45 PM

AI intellect generators are poisoned by a leftist-Marxist bent. Imagine holding a treat out for a dog.

<u>On Notice Words</u> 03/11/2025 03:59 PM

"They say" is an attraction treason like cologne.

<u>Albert Einstein Quote</u> 03/11/2025 05:21 PM

"Imagination is the language of the soul. Pay attention to your imagination and you will discover all you need to be fulfilled." Albert Einstein

<u>On Politics Inn</u> 03/11/2025 11:21 PM

Went to the "Politics Inn" for brunch. Ordered the Hypocrite Supreme meal, with a side order of corruption long fries and money laundered dressing on the side, and as an appetizer, taco chips with a bowl of hot fraud sauce. Oh, and a bottle of the House wine, Grifters.

<u>On Judges Unruly</u> 03/12/2025 04:17 PM Any Judges acting in bad faith should have decisions deemed null and void by Executive Order.

<u>On Appearances Viable</u> 03/12/2025 07:19 PM Best way to change appearance is a smile. Worst way is a frown.

<u>On Evil Biden</u> 03/12/2025 07:10 PM

Mephistopheles bought a mansion in heaven, and the U.S. citizen was forced to pay for it.

<u>On U.S.A. Democrat Ideology</u> 03/13/2025 03:11 PM Who commits the most crimes? Democrats. Crimes of theft, child trafficking, child maiming, rape, murder, vandalism, voter fraud, media propaganda lies which contribute to all the above and below, citizen persecution, onerous amounts of taxation, border invasions? Democrats. Money laundering, bribery, grifting, budget busting at the city, state, and federal levels? Democrats. Providing safe harbor to criminals? Democrats. We can live without them. Miseducation of children at all grade levels? Democrats. They are now soaked and drowning in their own lies and deceits and sold all of their lifeboats to the highest bidder.

<u>On Self-Analysis</u> 03/13/2025 01:55 PM

Too many people sabotage their own lives.

<u>On Climate Chicanery</u> 03/13/2025 06:47 PM Climate change hoaxers like Al Gore, Hollywood, John Kerry, United Nations, World Health Organization, world media, all education levels including elementary, college, and advanced sciences, marketeers, Big Tech companies, and every European Union country pushed this chaos upon world citizens only to acquire Marxist, leftist, totalitarian control of anything and everything planetary. Their driving forces of control, alleged moral high ground, and financial profits exposed the hoaxers as scoundrels nefarious. As idiots, they were declared heroes. Millions of more sentient people were tormented and preyed upon to never question and just bow to these corrupt people and more corrupt organizations.

<u>On Climate Hoaxers</u> 03/13/2025 07:24 PM

Save the planet. Give us your money.

<u>On Politics Puzzles</u> 03/14/2025 12:12 PM

When citizens complete the politics puzzle, what they see is corrupt politicians turned around, bent over, and pants down mooning us.

<u>On Sowell Wisdom</u> 03/14/2025 01:55 PM

"Activism is a way for useless people to feel important, even if the consequences of their activism are counterproductive for those they claim to be helping and damaging to the fabric of society as a whole." Thomas Sowell

<u>On the Politics Disease</u> 03/14/2025 03:16 PM

Corruption in politics is a pandemic.

<u>On Historic Times</u> 03/14/2025 11:23 PM

We live in the Age of Musk. We live in the Age of Trump. Perhaps one of the greatest and most vibrant ages of world History for politics and sciences innovations.

<u>On Adaptations</u> 03/14/2025 05:35 PM

The Big Tech age seems a bit scurrilous and complicated, but we continue to figure it out. The rout is on.

<u>On Media Salted Nuts</u> 03/14/2025 07:09 PM

Hey! I'm protesting you! Smash! Obviously, the physical smash is a crime. Or should we designate the media as the objects of protestation against the smashers? Media has fine-tuned smash and grab verbiage.

<u>On Pod Castings?</u> 03/15/2025 07:24 PM

What's so confusing during the setlines, Michelle? Maybe using the wrong bait?

<u>On Repetition Value</u> 03/16/2025 04:28 AM

If you reach your best effort and regularly maintain it, then it evolves into a habit.

<u>On Propaganda Bakes</u> 03/16/2025 03:05 PM

Half-truth combined with half-lie doesn't bake.

<u>On Leftists</u> 03/16/2025 11:42 PM

They don't deal in reason or reasonable. Spouting mindless mantras irrationally, for pay, does not a cake bake.

<u>On Song Era Favorites</u> 03/16/2025 11:52 PM

"Where The Streets Have No Name", U2. Covid Pandemic Era. Empty streets and empty people serving up empty purpose under empty government rule.

<u>On Biden Administration Corruption</u> 03/17/2025 07:44 PM

Federal government news, determined after audit: a female worker, after 8 months service, was fired, then paid $2,000,000 in severance pay! What in the hell did she do for 8 months, unsuccessfully, to merit such a severance payment? Citizen taxpayers would certainly like to know.

<u>On Judge Judgments</u> 03/18/2025 01:29 PM

How about we ignore the corrupt Judges. The media won't rebuke them. An unconstitutional ruling by a politically biased Judge is void during, after, and when the ruling is published.

<u>On Lingo</u> 03/18/2025 03:02 PM

Language is an art fart.

<u>On Politicians</u> 03/18/2025 03:19 PM

They tend to be squirrels' squirrels.

<u>On Political Holes</u> 03/18/2025 06:18 PM

Every politician has two holes. One between their face cheeks and one between their ass cheeks. (Repetition folks. For the memory hole.)

<u>On USA Judicial Matters</u> 03/18/2025 07:21 PM

If a judge issues a rogue order to obey or follow, then they have exceeded their constitutional authority, particularly when that judge ignores citizen rights and laws applicable to the issue at hand. The Executive Branch must not allow corrupt or bereft of morals judges to singularly rule this land.

<u>On Toasts</u> 03/19/2025 01:26 AM

May our dreams be sweet and you meals even sweeter.

<u>On Big Media Ops</u> 03/19/2025 11:31AM

Rarely do we hear Big Media knocking Stalin and Lenin. We wonder why when Stalin and Lenon seem to be the model for media propagandizing their government tenets.

<u>On Rogues</u> 03/19/2025 01:08 PM

Rogue judges should be treated like the rogues they are.

<u>On Understanding</u> 03/20/2025 02:04 AM

I'm not confused by Democrats. They will say and do anything to get elected and capture power, morals be damned. Once they are elected, they will say and do anything to keep that power. Proof is in the media pudding.

<u>On Fighting Politics</u> 03/20/2025 10:01 PM

USA politics has become a monumental battle between common sense and craziness.

<u>Russia 1917 & USA 2025</u> 03/20/2025 11:08 PM

The Russian Revolution of 1917 started on March 8 and ended on June 16, 1923. The USA Revolution started in March 2025 in earnest. Each revolution sought the same form of government: socialism.

<u>On Main Stream Media</u> 03/21/2025 12:07 AM

MSM is a puke show of inanity. Spewing out propaganda in every direction favoring their political buddies. A disgrace to journalism and TV broadcasting. They're hucksters and fraudsters. A hell of a messy dance.

<u>On Civilization Wrinkles</u> 03/21/2024 02:04 AM

Civilization should be much more civilized by now. We wreck and we build for generations on end. Repeat. Repeat. Repeat.

<u>On Mind Sparks</u> 03/21/2025 02:05 AM

Inspiration curious is inspiration spurious.

<u>On Judgment Ponderings</u> 03/21/2025 02:05 AM

Before judging someone else, judge yourself. A necessary reckoning moment.

<u>On Error Management</u> 03/21/2025 02:07 PM

Faults are often results of unsuspected stresses.

<u>On Sense Perceptions</u> 03/21/2025 02:10 AM

What our senses perceive is a product of our perceptions' maturity status. Similar moments, remembered after an aging process, are stages of "pulled up shades" understandings.

<u>On Decision Making</u> 03/21/2025 02:11 AM

Fear inhibits progress. A hurdle's height trips upward the failure possible. Practice jumping lower hurdles first, then through practice, progress from that point.

<u>On Boundary Hurdles</u> 03/21/2025 02:16 AM

An errant leap can be a perilous prospect. A successfully completed leap feels marvelous.

On Effort 03/21/2025 02:19 AM

No one moved an inch without first an inspiration tingle. Tickle of flesh contact or mind spark is an ignition for unfolding the movement mystery.

On Fear Factors 03/21/2025 02:25 AM

Fear response helps gauge frictions of life's pain.

On Bargains 03/21/2025 02:27 AM

A bargain is essentially a fictional reality providing a potential reality.

On Perfection Frauds 03/21/2025 02:30 AM

Some people believe they've never erred in life. These people should be avoided at all costs. They're life sustenance suckers, energy sappers, stealing the will of all living things around them.

On Law Equality 03/21/2025 02:36 AM

That equality exists under the law is a myth, a falsehood, a fiction. That the law is blind is not a compliment. It is an indictment. An insult to the rational mind.

On Rabble Causes 03/21/2025 02:39 AM

Rebellions of the guilty exercised against the innocent are crimes against nature.

On Mercy Decrees 03/21/2025 02:42 AM Mercey extended to lawbreakers is an irrational urge. No exceptions.

On Belief Variables 03/21/2025 02:43 AM

Faith is a myth but a comfortable one.

On Darkness Travails 03/21/2025 02:43 AM

Find yourself. No one really knows or cares that someone is lost.

On Age Degrees 03/21/2025 02:46 AM

I'd rather be old and wise than young and stupid.

On Friendships 03/21/2025 02:50 AM

Are friends advised or convenient?

<u>On Learning Relationships</u> 03/21/2025 02:52 AM

The young desperately need valuable learning experiences and not flakey fad-like unnecessaries.

<u>On Care Packages</u> 03/21/2025 02:53 AM

To care is to love. To not care is fakery.

<u>On Knowledge Deprivation</u> 03/21/2025 02:58 AM

To suffer under the weight of knowledge deprivation is a heavy burden to bear.

<u>On Knowledge Props</u> 03/21/2025 03:02 AM

Ignorance is shortened by knowledge until knowledge becomes shackled and rusted.

<u>On Mind Breaks Brakes</u> 03/21/2025 03:04 AM

A turned off mind is a spirit crusher.

<u>On Living Quirks/Quarks</u> 03/21/2025 03:07 AM

The self's best and worst inclinations are engaged in an eternal internal war of no resolution.

<u>On Bored Burns</u> 03/21/2025 03:09 AM

Monotony can relax the mind or stimulate random action possibilities.

<u>On Literary Inclinations</u> 03/21/2025 03:11 AM

For writers, pen to paper is a never ending temptation.

<u>On Energy Redemption</u> 03/21/2025 03:12 AM

Rest is needed despite time use drawbacks.

<u>On A Writer's Process</u> 03/21/2025 03:13 AM

Writers breathe thoughts and spit out ideas.

<u>On Poetic Brakes</u> 03/21/2025 03:15 AM

Ice is cold. Summer sidewalks are hot. Thoughts
get old. Desires do not.

<u>On Writing Tosses</u> 03/21/2025 03:18 AM

Writers throw ideas against the wall, then watch them dribble down as a story unfolds.

On Thoughting Serves 03/21/2025 03:22 AM

Even a stumbled upon thought is a trip worth taking.

On Rain Pain 03/21/2025 03:24 AM

It is a rainy night, and the mind feels the rainfall.

On Noisy Words 03/21/2025 03:26 AM

Every sound becomes a part of language lingo.

On Writing 03/21/2025 03:28 AM

Chained to thoughts at the wrist, trying to break free as the writing hand aches.

On Writing Sparks 03/21/2025 03:31 AM

Sometimes too many is too little, and too little is more than enough.

On Stock Investor Follies 03/21/2025 02:38 PM It isn't a far stretch to believe Wall Street investors of certain political bents intentionally tank market investment numbers, sell-sell-sell, then when stock prices go lower the mantra and actions become buy-buy-buy. They pick targets to tank depending on political, social, and religious views. 50 % to 60 % of these market mongrel revelations take place on regular mini or max scaling's.

English Literature on Facebook 03/21/2025 08:36 PM

"Poetry is the spontaneous overflow of powerful feelings: it takes its origin from emotion recollected in tranquility." William Wordsworth

On Reality Searches 03/21/2025 09:45 PM

Can't find the truth if you don't look for it.

On IRS Efficiency 03/21/2025 10:48 PM

USA Internal Revenue Service is 30 years behind schedule on a project that was supposed to be completed in 6 years. Oddly enough, the project was intended to make more efficient monitoring and review of citizen taxation forms. The project has still not been completed, exceeding the original project funding amount by 15 billion dollars!

<u>On Judge Procrastination</u> 03/22/2025 01:49 PM

New USA Federal Judge corruption looks like this: a decision "stay", or delay, is put on issue resolution. A warrant is issued against those who protest the stay. These Judges aren't acting like Judges. They are acting like saboteurs. At the Federal level, the President's Executive and Administrative Branches, under the Constitution, hold equal power and weight with the Judicial and Legislative Branches. Therefore, if a Federal Judge decides to delay a decision on an important and relevant National issue, the already existing affairs of State remain legal, viable, and available. The law hasn't been changed yet, so there is nothing to be appealed. The Executive Branch can proceed as it intended without distraction or prevention. It is not required to wait for the mollycoddlers of Federal resistance to act.

<u>On Restaurant Menus</u> 03/22/2025 01:55 PM

Judges and journalists are now eating at the "Bottom of the Barrel" restaurant.

<u>On Judge Jerks</u> 03/22/2025 02:00 PM If a citizen poses a question to another citizen, and the question isn't ever answered, then nothing related to the question's purpose has factually changed. In other words, Judges can't freeze reality. (Seems some of these Judges use comic books to make decisions.)

<u>On Doors</u> 03/22/2025 02:22 PM

Hinges are neither sacred nor permanent.

<u>On Presidents</u> 03/22/2025 02:29 PM

Biden was a high maintenance jalopy. Trump is a Rolls Royce.

<u>On Citizen Survival</u> 03/22/2025 02:36 PM

The U.S. citizen is like the penny that rolls around on the sidewalk, kicked around, stepped upon, then finally ends up in the hand of a homeless person who really needs and appreciates it.

<u>On Knowing</u> 03/22/2025 02:49 PM

To learn is to know, but knowing is an amorphous entity.

<u>On Edgy Wedgy Govs and Citz</u> 03/22/2025 03:18 PM Fuck you all! Fuck you all. Your squawkin' and your talkin' make you small.

The hennin' and the pennin' take a fall, while the stupids and the ign'rant make a call.

Fuck you all! Fuck you all. FUCK YOU ALLLLL!

(Boink)

(Sometimes these tunes write themselves.) (Govs = Rulers; Citz = citizens ditzy.) (listening to a WBJC radio Opera presentation while writing this ditty-doo-doo.)

You can call it naughty, or you can call it nice. You can call it haughty, or you can call it thrice. Still not commin' back to the shack.

<u>On U.S. Supremes Reflections 9</u> 03/22/2025 03:35 PM Someone tell the U.S. Supreme Court to get their heads out of their asses. (Emergency crews standing by.)

<u>On Required Suggested Learnings</u> 03/22/2025 04:05 PM Seems the Kama Sutra has become required and popular reading for modern day 5th graders around the world. After all, seeming is believing.

<u>On Perspectives</u> 03/22/2025 04:07 PM Watch horror movies to witness a better reflection of the world of men, women, and all of the bots and creatures.

<u>On Life</u> 03/22/2025 04:16 PM

Life is an occupation. (Think of it what you will. Make of it what you want. Lots of holes and pitfalls. Wear decent shoes.)

<u>On Expressions</u> 03/22/2025 04:34 PM

There's a first way, a second way, and an anyway.

<u>On Changes</u> 03/22/2025 05:15 PM

Change is sometimes faked. Back many years ago, we didn't know what we didn't know. Now, we know more than we could have imagined.

<u>On Democracy Haunts</u> 03/22/2025 05:17 PM

Democrats, in effect, are now the pompous clown party.

<u>On Politician Tongues</u> 03/22/2025 05:23 PM

Baltimore's Mayor recently said student education isn't as bad as we've been told. Citizens know it is worse than they've been told. Paying for failure is generational in Baltimore.

<u>On Protest Industry</u> 03/22/2025 05:34 PM

Protesting is an economic industry unto itself.

<u>On Reality Ticks</u> 03/22/2025 07:46 PM

Experience says reality fails. It just depends on however long it lasts as a gauge of happiness and weariness. Tragedy always wants to siren itself in between possibilities. Not a bogus bit of nuance allowed or invited to loosen a fix.

<u>On Baseball Season</u> 03/23/2025 03:37 PM

On the cusp of Baseball Season openers, we pause and reflect upon the emotional feathers and faints that will be faced on the diamond space.

<u>On Info Overload</u> 03/23/2025 04:36 PM

When it comes to consuming information, consider the source, always.

<u>Shadows Within My Mind</u> on Facebook 03/23/2025 04:39 PM

"Keep the real ones close. Ain't too many left." Tupac Shakur

"I can't believe what you say, because I see what you do." James Baldwin

<u>English Literature</u> on Facebook 03/23/2025 04:45 PM

"I still don't know how to work out a poem. A poem needs understanding through the senses. The point of diving into a lake is not immediately to swim to the shore, but to be in the lake to luxuriate in the sensation of water. You do not work the lake out, it is an experience beyond thought. Poetry soothes and emboldens the soul to accept the mystery." John Keats

"A life spent making mistakes is not only more honorable, but more useful than a life spent doing nothing." George Bernard Shaw

<u>On Politics</u> 03/24/2025 05:15 AM

A political party of no morals and no credibility is no party at all.

<u>On Corrupt Judges</u> 03/24/2025 09:22 AM

The current USA leftist Judges' corral has usurped the USA constitution by imposing laws upon citizens never contemplated or contemplated and not passed and were rejected by Congress. These Judges' actions are unlawful, immoral, and totalitarian in nature. Nature rejects them. These Judases should be banished from work in the legal systems. They are a plague upon land, sea, and air.

<u>Shadows Within My Mind</u> on Facebook 03/25/2025 02:28 PM

"We can disagree and still love each other, unless your disagreement is rooted in my oppression and denial of my humanity and right to exist." James Baldwin

"If you don't believe in freedom of speech for people you disagree with, you don't believe in freedom of speech at all." Noam Chomsky

<u>On Seasons' Changes</u> 03/26/2025 03:33 AM

Winter, spring, summer, and fall, moves lull, some all. Seasons come, seasons go, all in a single row. Sometimes early, sometimes late, not married to a single date. In and out, up and down; heat, wind, wild air, and cold. Ancient as the seasons' bold.

<u>On Unrequited Love</u> 03/26/2025 04:18 AM

When in love, the ache of not a single touch becomes difficult to take or accept. Distractions are sought, but eventually they become doused in a certain glass of fate. Numbed are these emotions, or diverted through work of mind and body until each are fraught with an exhaustion calming. Writing and reading serve as a relaxing salve and massaging soft balm. Sleep is the tomb for love unrequited. Just another sidestep around emotions blighted. Unresolved satisfactions come in many forms. All can be resolved by a practiced resolve. None may seem of immediate help, but the efforts themselves put the mind into a deference remorse healthy.

On Musings Futures 03/27/2025 01:57 AM

The days of wisdom have long ago passed, and the only trail viable is a journey to the past. A one way ticket to where lonely is the light, and holy is the night.

On Democrats 03/27/2025 03:49 AM

It seems USA Democrats claimed a dubious right to destroy us all as payback for their political losses.

On Uselessness 03/27/2025 03:51 AM

Where is the mind when the brain is lost? In a place of glossy costs. Bling be praised. Sense be lost.

On Energy Strains 03/27/2025 03:54 AM

I see the faces of those who inspired me. I hear the voices of those who tired me. A see-saw balancing act emotionally. The final tip curious.

On Love Laws 03/27/2025 11:55 PM

What we do for love is what we need to do for love to survive. Driven by desire or chore, love lives to restore.

On Seasons 03/28/2025 12:07 AM

Springtime and baseball are complimentary passion ignitions.

On A Good Life 03/28/2025 07:13 AM

Honesty and morals have become a long dead concept in this world.

On Tit for Tat 03/28/2025 09:25 AM

If citizens treated politicians the way politicians treat them, the politicians would no longer exist.

<u>On Planned Perfection</u> 03/29/2025 01:46 AM

Practice approaches perfection when a plan implemented is precisely targeted towards improvement of skills needed to achieve planned goals.

<u>On Trust Fences</u> 03/29/2025 12:09 PM

Trust is a key ingredient in a relationship amidst all creatures. When it's gone, it never comes back.

<u>On Life Currency</u> 03/29/2025 12:35 PM

We all die alone, so it is best to get used to yourself along the way.

<u>On Knowledge Caches</u> 03/29/2025 12:43 PM

Books are a human extension of the mind, on paper. AI is an extension of the mind, on computers, and sometimes on paper. All knowledge in the human mind comes from a human mind able to observe life and then attach a meaning to it through learning from other humans, creatures, land, sea, books, and in the 21st century, AI created by humans.

<u>On Extensions</u> 03/29/2025 12:47 PM

"Buts" are an extension of the literary mind. "Toilets" are an extension of the biology mind.

<u>On the Life Test</u> 03/29/2025 12:58 PM

All creatures great and small start as an experiment. Life and growth elements are added to the experiment. Results may vary according to ingredients added, how much added, and when added.

<u>On Perspective</u> 03/29/2025 01:34 PM

Every life has a perspective, and stories connected to it.

<u>On Priority</u> 03/29/2025 03:01 PM

Need versus want is a battle that destroys the living of many.

<u>On Life Hurts</u> 03/29/2025 03:03 PM

Truth and lies battle with flies.

<u>On Writing</u> 03/29/2025 03:07 PM

Writing is a misery necessary.

<u>On Outer Space Trips</u> 03/29/2025 05:06 PM

Given the organ damage possible during long outer space travels, for example, from Earth to Mars, can a mini-magnetic field be created to surround or encase the spaceship to protect the passengers from organ destruction triggered by biological and chemical alterations of the human body? Portable magnetic field generators? Could developed drugs help maintain normal kidney functions? Reference: Earth.com, "Nature Communications" Journal.

<u>On Happy</u> 03/30/2025 03:37 AM

Arrive happy. Be happy. Call happy. Day happy. Each happy. Fail happy. Gray happy. Hale happy. Ill happy. Jam happy. Kind happy. Live happy. Mail happy. Nail happy. Old happy. Puppy happy. Quiet happy. Rule happy. Sail happy. Trail happy. Urge happy. Vie happy. Wake happy. Xylophone happy. Zoo happy.

<u>On Media Mushes</u> 03/30/2025 12:50 PM

It's pretty clear the major media news and subsets are in the business of fiction broadcasting and publishing. Facts and truths appear as accidental tourists.

<u>On Media Banshees</u> 03/30/2025 05:05 PM

In this day and age, one wonders just how many lies and deceits will be produced by the banshees of media.

<u>On Weddings</u> 03/30/2025 05:45 PM

Wed leads to eye dew. Wed leads to bye, too. Wed leads to "Hi", boo. Wed leads to bind hue. Wed leads to say "I do". Wed leads to buy who. Wed leads to try, too. Wed leads to rye, sue. Wed leads to strive, blue. Wed leads to why, too. Wed leads to where ware. Wed leads to owe, too. Wed leads to row through.

<u>On Human Worth</u> 03/30/2025 06:15 PM

Humans could basically be characterized by nature as walking, talking, singing, blinging, laughing, crying, rioting, whining, puking, disgusting, skanky turd shit. Still, if allowed, they fertilize the ground upon death.

On Time Bents 03/31/2025 02:34 AM

To leave or not to leave. That is the question. To escape the rat race, the too fast pace, and not seek fame and fortune, but merely a quieter place of much less proportion. Or, apply the paste, and not flame out or misfortune, but merely find a quitter place of much more distortion.

On Poor Philosophy 03/31/2025 02:36 AM

Less is more if only you stay poor.

On Aimless Travels 03/31/2025 02:38 AM

Tracks and treks of no sound and no rest are nothing but less fest.

On Matters Liquid 03/31/2025 02:46 AM

An ocean is like a desert in that each has undrinkable waters.

On Physics Phobia 03/31/2025 02:49 AM

In life, no exact center exists. It is a fax figment of perfection.

On Time Tunnels 03/31/2025 02:51 AM

While racing backwards in time, he realized he was traveling to nowhere.

On Wisdom Knocks 03/31/2025 02:55 AM

Conventional wisdom is a fools road.

On Political Sharts 03/31/2025 10:57 AM

The USA Democratic Party has perfected imperfection. They've gone back to the Cloward-Piven radical plan: resist, riot, revolution. But they now just call it protesting. "Ignore those burning buildings and vandalized businesses. They're nothingburgers."

On Politics Ticks 03/31/2025 12:26 PM

Politicians become the local poison wherever they go.

On Easter Reflections 03/31/2025 12:29 PM

That cross the 1829 Democrats built to nail upon anyone not them has become, in the 21ˢᵗ century, the cross they've been nailing themselves onto. Turnabout is fair play.

On Special Places 03/31/2025 12:32 PM

It's a long road to Martha's Vineyard. The road leads to where politicians die.

On Day Streams 03/31/2025 12:46 PM

It's a warm and sunny day of slight winds, birds chirping, bees humming, insects flying around, bugs exploring all manner of places in the neighborhood. A Spring of sense and nonsense plenty.

On Gender Views 03/31/2025 01:33 PM

40 genders plus subsets. Tools and fools of sum

doom abound. A gender is not an opinion. It is a biological fact. Take a biology class and relieve the mind of shit.

On Politicians 03/31/2025 01:50 PM

By and large, politicians hate audits as they despise accountability.

On April Fools Day 04/01/2025 00:00 All Day

It's that day again and I have no ideas whatsoever of time and what to write. Oh wait, April Fools.

On Truth Tenets 04/01/2025 05:15 AM

Truth has a voice whether masked, vanquished, vanished, or banished. Once spoken, written, or musically sounded out, it lives forever and a day. No absolutes exist, but truth comes closest to seeking and finding absolution. Neither magic nor closed curtains can contain it.

On Pardons 04/01/2025 05:19 AM

May I seek a pardon from errant ways. May many lives live better days.

On Time Annoys Noise 04/01/2025 05:23 AM

Which first sounded? A tick or the tock of a clock?

<u>On Politicians</u> 04/01/2025 11:58 AM

Is the USA Democrat Party a serial killer? Check their murder stats across the country in cities, counties, and towns.

<u>On Days in Progress</u> 04/01/2025 01:29 PM

Every day presents a search for meaning.

<u>On Self Destruction</u> 04/01/2025 03:31 PM

Useful idiots. Marketeers, advertisers love them. If one wants to achieve financial security, then don't be a useful idiot throwing too much money at them. Prioritize needs over wants. Wants can wait.

<u>On Devil Deals</u> 04/01/2025 08:07 PM

Devil's in the details. That's why politicians intentionally leave out the poisonous details.

<u>On World Views</u> 04/02/2025 04:02 PM

If looking at this world with a neutral mindset, it can better be described, regardless of weather conditions, by just how dark it has become.

<u>On Crows' Haunts</u> 04/03/2025 01:58 PM

There's a crow outside my window perched upon

an electric wire across the street, seeking truth and solace amidst all nature and natures.

<u>On Propaganda Wars</u> 04/04/2025 03:58 PM

The USA public education people are growing kids up to become misery merchants.

<u>On Tariff Wars</u> 04/04/2025 04:00 PM

The Democrat Party is all in on using the tariff wars as another political scheme to avert eyes away from their avowed corruptions.

<u>On Story Origins</u> 04/04/2025 05:46 PM

Every single fictions or fantasy story is based in historical facts and legends passed down generationally.

<u>On Maryland Humans</u> 04/05/2025 05:00 PM

Maryland politicians are some of the most corrupt in the country, so any tax hikes passed means they are stealing more money for themselves so they can control how it is used, instead of the individual citizens deciding how to use it. The politicians are surely not better keepers of the wealth flame. Their antics have been allowed to go on much too long.

<u>Shadows Within My Mind</u> on Facebook 04/05/2025 07:20 PM

"We don't even ask happiness, just a little less pain. Charles Bukowski

"What is a rebel? A man who says no." Albert Camus.

<u>On Informaphobes</u> 04/05/2025 07:36 PM

People who get mentally knockout-punched when they realize they were utterly completely wrong. They refuse to accept such a reality realization and will ridiculously resolve to argue otherwise. Example: someone who fears the truth, suffers truth spasms, then makes miserable those who do know the truth.

<u>On Mind Bends</u> 04/06/2025 03:16 AM

Don't let the mind fool you. It is usually a devious stunt to avoid a truth despised.

<u>On Book Reading Decline</u> 04/06/2025 04:53 AM

Recently read a story on my mobile phone which says, in general, people don't read books much anymore. I disagree. "War and Peace" by Leo Tolstoy is about 1,300 pages long. The average Christian "Holy Bible" is about the same amount of pages. The average Holy Arabic "Quran" is 604 pages. The average Hebrew Bible "Tanakh" is about 1,574 pages. The average Hinduism Holy Books of the "Vedas" are about 9,500 pages. The Buddhist Holy Book "Tipitaka" is over 12,000 pages.

Just considering these Holy Books, which are read or reread in varied parts of the world on an almost daily basis, it appears plenty of reading is consumed then contemplated. Science books can be categorized similarly. Fantasy and fiction books can also be characterized similarly. "How-To-Do" books can be characterized similarly, too. Same for Children's books.

There is more than a plentiful amount of reading books happenings all over the world. Books can now be accessed, or listened to audibly, on mobile phones, computer tablets and desktops, or in libraries at work or school. The intellectual impact of such knowledge availability has somewhat become a white noise due to such high amounts of reading at any cost. It is tree leaves responding to a wind kiss. Radio and television are also still available for intellectual consumption.

My guess is the author's concern was whether the viability, sensibility, availability, and reliability of reading and listening materials were adequately served and dined upon by the public at large.

On Politics Math 04/06/2025 05:20 PM

Republicans = my way or the highway + go along to get along.

Democrats = socialists + liberals + leftists + Marxists + Fascists.

On Jest Human Characteristics 04/06/2025 10:21 PM

In jest, the four lifetime personalities are: optimist; pessimist; optimistic pessimist; pessimistic optimist. And if you want to Zuckerberg it further, try varied jesterations (new word) of 40 plus more characteristics.

On Party Poopers 04/07/2025 04:32 AM

The Democrat politicians were invited to the party, accepted the invitation, then attempted to turn it into a miserable experience for all who attended. Who does that?!?

On Propaganda Influences 04/07/2025 10:48 PM

We just witnessed in real time the manipulation of the global stock markets: a TV network was allegedly informed the Trump administration will announce a 90 -day pause on the raised tariff price imposed upon foreign nations to counter the tariff rip-offs politicians going back to Nixon allowed to maintain "good" relations. Seriously. Pursuing a favorable rating from a totalitarian government because they employed so many workers at pittance prices to make the products Americans wanted more than needed. The quality of those products was of little concern to the politicians.

After the TV network false story was reported, the US stock market immediately skyrocketed in value. The Trump administration contacted the TV network and told them the story wasn't true. It was reported as not true, then the US stock market suffered a major selling crash, one of the largest dollar amount crashed in US history. What was witnessed by the audience of citizens wondering about the viability of their life savings accounts turned out to be a classic criminal insider trading manipulation scheme, and one very familiar to stock market managers and politicians, who it seems were all in on it. They've gone too far. Simply, too far, now at the point of no return.

On "Studies" 04/07/2025 12:49 PM

Every "study", regardless of science or economic origin, is infected by the human mind virus called "bias". The bias must be analyzed to understand the magnitude of the study perspective.

On Rational Rotted 04/08/2025 07:24 AM

Two wrongs do not make a right just as two rights aren't necessarily any better than one wrong.

On Government Wastes 04/09/2025 02:47 AM

The government wouldn't need so much of my money if they were not ardent illicit distributers of the money forcibly taken.

On Sleep Slavery 04/09/2025 03:25 AM Sleep is a human necessity, but it leaves the mind and body exposed and surrendered to all surfaces, all airs, and all hazards the world environments and enchantments impose.

On Wall Street Blues 04/09/2025 11:33 AM

Seems the Wall Street numbers, on a daily basis, indicate U.S. investors trust their own country much more, in general, than they trust foreign ones. Shall I go into the history of why this feeling exists?

On Brit Brain 04/09/2025 11:39 AM

"Don't let the peasants keep too much of their money or they will become self-serving and powerful", says every politician in every country in every world. Exceptions are rare.

On Hackers 04/09/2025 11:45 AM

Hacking should be considered a capital crime. Hunt those bastards and bitches down and put us out of their misery.

On Tot Mons 04/09/2025 11:55 AM

The Democrats are not in favor of democracy. They are totalitarian in nature monsters. Tot Mons.

On Human Ignitions 04/09/2024 12:16 PM

Democrats are attracted to money. Republicans are attracted to morality.

On Wall Street Wars 04/09/2025 12:21 PM

President Trump's re-election ignited the Wall Street Wars. Everyone who invests in the markets is a finance soldier.

On Tariff Wars 04/09/2025 12:34 PM

At least the U.S. economy is now armed, dangerous, and firing back at the foreign nations' blitzkrieg. Sure, it's a tariff war, and General Trump has rallied the U.S. citizen investors to fight back. To the victors go the spoils.

On Government Waste / Fraud 04/09/2025 12:43 PM

Too many government agencies must be quashed and restructured or eliminated. Their waste and fraud actions are beyond abominable. Examples: IRS, FBI, CIA, every Pentagon agency, every SSA (Social Security Administration) agency, EPA, the Department of Education agency, and many more on the chopping block. The

Democrat-run news organizations are apoplectic over these proceedings. Guessing they will miss their kickback money.

<u>On Government Tyranny</u> 04/09/2025 12:53 PM

Be happy or be prosecuted. Such is the fate of every citizen.

<u>On Stock Markets Flex</u> 04/09/2025 01:52 PM

In real time, I'm looking at the largest percentage Stock Market gains in 60 plus years.

<u>On Roots Human</u> 04/09/2025 02:07 PM

The roots of harmony live amidst roots of chaos. It takes a noble soul to work on growing those roots into a harmony tree. Congrats to all women who have learned and instituted lessons upon us. We are better humans, worldwide, for it.

<u>On Truth Effect</u> 04/09/2025 02:27 PM

Truth is a freedom lance and launcher.

<u>On Wisdom Searches</u> 04/09/2025 02:47 PM

Quick to judge and poor to reason is a miserable way to live.

<u>On Time Degrees</u> 04/09/2025 02:51 PM

The moment of time influences the needs of necessity. Time has a scale much like weighted measures.

<u>On Propaganda Panda's</u> 04/09/2025 03:11 PM

The Democrat media mostly Captains the ship "Propaganda". It's been run aground, and mostly unmovable at this moment of the 21st century.

<u>On Gas Shortages</u> 04/09/2025 03:15 PM

Sometimes, chaos and bullshit are the only fuels available.

<u>On Presidents</u> 04/09/2025 03:32 PM

President 47 is a once in a lifetime leader. He has defended U.S. citizens against all odds and ill-intended aggressors. I sleep much better at night. Able to fight off the demoncrat dreams.

<u>On Hells Angels</u> 04/09/2025 06:17 PM

Hells virgins can terrorize terrorists.

<u>On University Terrorists</u> 04/09/2025 06:19 PM

Terrorists administratively rule Ivy League U's.

<u>On The View</u> 04/09/2025 06:21 PM

The Hosts of the show are blithering idiots x 5.

<u>On China Syndrome</u> 04/09/2025 07:07 PM

"We're not China" is a badge of honor.

<u>On Leftist Ideals</u> 04/09/2025 07:32 PM

Their chants are rants. Never take fools advice.

<u>On Freshness</u> 04/09/2025 09:17 PM

Fresh hell beats stale hell.

<u>On Overdue Process</u> 04/09/2025 10:17 PM

Due process exists at the tip of a bullet when it comes to prosecuting drug dealing cartels.

<u>On 75 Pins Bowling</u> 04/09/2025 11:07 PM

President 47 Trump played tenpins with 75 pins standing and knocked down 74 pins with the role of his first ball. The remaining pin still standing now understands it is merely a spare.

<u>On Loose Hairs</u> 04/10/2025 04:55 AM

They are prone to attempts at escape from the natural body. Whether escape is meant as a mere freedom attempt is uncertain. Freedom starts as empowerment. What's next is sole responsibility for one's actions. Freedom's choice: whether to serve needs or to serve wants. That choice leads to many potential pitfalls. Strike a balance. Rise or fall. Prosperity or poverty awaits. Choices really matter.

<u>On Political Idiocracy</u> 04/10/2025 10:27 PM

Why do Democrats persecute Republicans for being successful? Jealousy?

<u>On Perspectives</u> 04/11/2025 02:39 AM

Some people see the world as it is. Some people see the world and wonder. Some people see the world as they wish it to be. Some as it could be. Some as it shouldn't be. Some as it couldn't be. Regardless, each looks at it like a bee. Too much to see is too much to be.

On Partnership Love 04/11/2025 04:29 AM

Romantic love seems more like a false feeling. Romance without a friendship feeling is just a sexual urge, a feeling inbred, the purpose of it is to propagate more of the human species whether purposely or accidentally. To simplify, gay love is similar in need and desire minus the species propagation aspect. Thus, the biology of love is quite a simple equation.

In the biology world, genders are a laughable fantasy furthered by body manipulation surgically. When such surgery is perpetrated against minors, then civil rights have been chilled, and a crime has been committed.

Now, it's proposed that recorded hospital births are not identified as just male or female, but they should also include unknown. If the hospital is unable to determine the sex of a newborn, then that place shouldn't be operating as a hospital at all. "Unknown" is a crime against the child.

Raising a child as an unknown sex is a crime against humanity. It is a barbaric practice meant to control the child's sexual fate, then further abused as a premise for sex reversal. Sex reversal is not biologically possible. It is nothing but plastic surgery designed to disguise the child as a different sex being. All the parties involved in this type of body mutilation should be prosecuted for crimes against the child.

I can think of no worse way to raise a child. Raise to remain uncertain of their biology? What, is it a secret that only parents and hospitals can discover and reveal? Essentially, all around this child, including teachers, have conspired to choose a gender for the child. Abominable.

On Mailbox Ad Mailers 04/11/2025 05:12 PM

Democrat Party = throwaway Mailer garbage Ads.

<u>On Basic Sense</u> 04/11/2025 05:22 PM

Basically, all of these Democrat Party politician complaints about president 47 are based in their own sore lack of common sense. Perhaps their money laundering senses have been insulted.

<u>On Cartels Domestic</u> 04/11/2025 04:40 PM

The activists groups are literal cartels. Riot and mayhem pushers. Also known by the name "terrorists".

<u>On Nudism's</u> 04/11/2025 05:43 PM

The Democrat Party has completely exposed their hypocrisy like a nudist running down the middle of a public street.

<u>On The Biden Legacy</u> 04/11/2025 05:52 PM

Coin flips and dirty rice is no way to run a country.

<u>On Life Trekking</u> 04/11/2025 06:03 PM

There are various times in one's life when a decision must be made: whether to continue the same path or seek out and learn about another path. Hopefully, after finding a path most compatible with one's personality, desires, and learned skills, then the path's end will stare back as a peaceable, comfortably furnished, approachable porch or front stoop.

<u>On Turd Smell Philosophy</u> 04/11/2025 06:08 PM

Turds long and hard stink large. Suddenly, politicians and car dealers come to mind.

<u>On Gambling Sins</u> 04/11/2025 06:18 PM

Like gamblers who risk other people's money, once politicians learn they can get away with financial corruption crimes, they become addicted to such purpose and activity.

<u>On Writing</u> 04/11/2025 06:21 PM Waiting begets writing like breathes beget breathes.

<u>On DoGE Audits</u> 04/11/2025 08:57 PM

DoGE it or lose it forever.

<u>On Destiny Haunts</u> 04/11/2025 09:47 PM

The U.S.A. must control their own destiny or that destiny will be destruction.

<u>On Purity Reality</u> 04/13/2025 02:07 AM

There's nothing pure in this world. It's a messed up situation. No wars and no patience can resolve it.

Bridges collapse and towers fall. No god dare claim responsibility for it all.

What a waist this spite and taste. A dystopian fantasy in this place.

So, give me a smoke and pass me a beer, then hire an Uber ride to a clean, happy space dear.

No need to run. No need to race. Slow and steady wins the chase. Just another belch, piss, and shit to erase.

Every one of the human species ever born and lived long enough amongst a mentally sterile population can confirm the incredulous waste.

Courage, courage. Not only a word.

Our Sun star keeps alive enough. It's emitted rays have burned this race, tempered by earth's magnetic field, prevents the planet from raw meat eating disgrace.

So, cheer up, button up, rest. Exercise, eat smart. Offer smiles genuine to others in the race. Moaning and groaning about farts only brings sorrows. If lucky, there will exist many tomorrows.

Even the friendliest faces and voices harbor ill-intentioned choices. Get over it. It will get over you.

<u>On Memory Day-Frames</u> 04/13/2025 11:23 PM

Been wondering and wandering about night time to early morning dreams while sleeping. Why do just snippets of reality memory scenes come and go, as I, the character seen from a body uncertain in a place where mirrors are scarce, move about slowly, observing and listening, sometimes interacting with others in the dream known from the past, some near faceless or not confronted face to face. I can identify some of the other characters, but some are unknown to me or perhaps unfamiliar to memory.

After many years of these played out dream scenes, I decided to write down as much about the scenes in descriptive form, not judging them, but recording them pen to paper while awake. Accumulated quite a few and parked them in my memory, ready to let them ride around in the night time dream slip world. The purpose was to search for meaning. Read a few dreams books along the way during awake time to also learn the purpose and pathways of each dream sequences.

To start, I've been writing quite a lot about my own dreams since about 5 years old, planning to become a writer since that time. Seemed like a good use of my life. To shy at the time to speak out loud much, I wrote down what was observed and experience, summarized form of days or weeks, sometimes too busy in life entanglements and skipped the process for months, but in the teen years, the records seemed much more relevant because I feared losing the memories.

Every written fantasy book is comprised of real experiences morphed into fantasy characters who tell the story, whether they are humans or other forms of creatures of the land, sky, or sea. The author is the dream watcher, helping the characters to move about and communicate. Recently, in my 60's era of age, it became time to figure out just what had happened in my mind over many years. What influenced it, how did I respond to the influences?

So, I tasked myself with day dreaming. Translating mentally the night dream scenes into life snippets, and also transforming reality life scenes into dream-like snippets. On my first test, I was able to recall seconds of snippets of my life in seconds long photographs in my mind, much like comic book framed illustrations. It worked.

The scenes flipped in and around in a two dimensional loop from my childhood and up to the time I first met the woman who I would eventually marry. I timed this time frame at 15 to 20 seconds. Yes, that quickly did seemingly relevant snippets appear. Maybe try this next time I run over a writing road bump. There are great stories hiding everywhere. Just flush them out the darkness.

<u>On Reality Bumps</u> 04/14/2025 03:28 AM

If life is lived long enough, it occurs that we are random selections in a birth lottery. The meaning of life is varied, random. Better than nothing.

<u>On Parallels</u> 04/15/2025 12:43 PM

J.K. Rowling, from a political perspective, wrote one of the ultimate parallels to a corrupt political system terrorizing the citizenry when her pen first touched paper to write the Harry Potter book series. Right up there with J.R.R Tolkien's "Lord of the Rings", Frank Herbert's "Dune", and Robert E. Howard's Solomon Kane.

<u>On Tax Day</u> 04/15/2025 12:51 PM

It's here. Greedy governments favorite day. Taxes due. File your papers or sleep in a jail. Tax day perfectly personifies corrupt governments and those who favor corrupt governments.

<u>On Basic Economics</u> 04/15/2025 01:05 PM

Citizens don't cause recessions. Politicians, corrupt

Donors, and supporters do. Recession mongers exist, corruptly.

<u>On Devils Dancing</u> 04/15/2025 01:57 PM

The devil's in the details means those of a will to do harm exist, and today, in larger numbers than any time in world history. Learn the devils means and methods to help develop skills of resistance to this plague, then squash it.

<u>On Goodness Morals</u> 04/15/2025 02:15 PM

Good citizens resist corrupt government.

<u>On Life Dice Rolls</u> 04/15/2025 02:22 PM

We're all odds makers. Sometimes it's better to go with the odds and sometimes it's worse. Even sour pickles offer a tempting taste.

<u>On Modern Medicine</u> 04/15/2025 05:54 PM

Cure for insomnia: playback of any Kamala Harris speech from the last 5 years. Works masterfully.

<u>On IRS Intrigues</u> 04/15/2025 06:03 PM

In 2021, it was determined that 149,000 federal Internal Revenue Service workers didn't file and pay their taxes.

<u>On Political Poop Battles</u> 04/16/2025 03:31 PM

Trump 47-Day 86

Fed Chair Powell comes out guns blazing today in Chicago, trying to nip in the bud any citizen efforts to make a better life for themselves and families who have suffered 4 years of Powell/Biden, accompanied by Generals Pelosi and Shumer, economic sabotage efforts. Meanwhile, recently elected President 47 has ordered his troops to step up efforts to prepare for these Napoleonic failed Battle of Waterloo circumstances by ordering preparation of "Waste Treatment Plant" island accommodations for Powell/Biden and their Generals. May their final "Saint Helena Island" days stink to high hell.

<u>On Freedom</u> 04/17/2025 03:59 AM

There is only one true freedom, and it is freedom of choice, whether it be good, bad, or indifferent.

<u>On Idiots of This World</u> 04/17/2025 04:49 AM

Some kids on the playground decided to play a pickup game of basketball. Two captains were chosen, then each captain started to make their picks in alternative order. Each captain picked the best player available during each pick. Neither of them decided their pick based on race, color, or religious creed. The goal was to win, and not to feel good about the picks.

On Politician Responsibility 04/17/2025 12:59 PM

On a daily basis, politicians fail to remember their only purpose in that job is to serve the citizens who "legally" elected them. Anything else but that one purpose is irrelevant.

On Crazy Loons: Media 04/17/2025 01:50 PM

Media are largely half-sentient loons bent on keeping populations grossly ill-informed.

On Nation Self-destruction 04/17/2025 06:07 PM

These nations who are empowering Communist Chinese leaders are knowingly empowering their own doom in exchange for money. Doom is still doom no matter how the coins roll.

On Joe Biden, Serial Killer 04/17/2025 06:17 PM

As U.S. President, Joe Biden led invasions of our

borders by thousands of criminals. He's a serial killer.

On Media Nonsense 04/17/2025 11:58 PM

They're gettin' better at not being bad. Grudgingly.

On Good Nights 04/18/2025 04:48 PM

One last thing to write before I say goodnight. It's gonna' be alright. It's gonna' be alright.

On Astronautish Joy 04/18/2025

Six women took a joy ride on a space rocket, then one of them, after the return trip, claimed being an Astronaut was an interesting experience. Someone tell her a tourist passenger doesn't qualify a person as a pilot.

On The Shadows 04/19/2025 04:27 AM

In the Sun's daylight he mourned for the shadows. They scurried away in retreat. A traveler, on the other hand, meandered by and could find solace in the shadows. A refreshing coolness abounded behind the shadows curtain. Aloneness became cleansing to the mind and soul there. A solace place to placate the Sun's invasions.

On Clock Tricks 04/19/2025 04:55 AM

A clock's tic can produce a foolhardy emotional excursion upon senses random reacting to movements, moans, and groans similar in motion and sounds to sexual dances up, down, and finally, loud bursts of satisfactions and lonely regrets.

On Discretion 04/19/2025 08:30 PM

People who don't like facts are not worth knowing about and not worth worrying about.

On Reality Checks 04/19/2025 08:45 PM

Don't be afraid to face reality. Reality isn't afraid to face you.

On Answers 04/20/2025 12:35 PM

You're welcome is your welcome. Well done job is not well done meat. Early severance is an unconnected securance. Reverence is ir-reverence. To want is a need unwanted. To need is a want unneeded. Doing nothing is nothing doing. There's a "heard" and those who are herded. To be or not to be is a dumb query. You never know until you no. A cake can look good, but the taste crosses the finish line as grace or waste. Angry is energy wild; happy is energy mild. No one is stamped with knowledge at birth; it must painfully be learned. To despair of all hope is to live life as a sick joke. To be happy with little money parallels to be miserable with much money. To love is a queer thought. Love has many definitions and meanings, and in-volves many practices, all skewed by personality flaws.

On Answers More 04/20/2025 12:55 AM

Many days for many ways and many ways for many days. Girl, boy; woman, man; simple and divine biology mined. If you want to hear a thought, then listen for it to seen and grow. Never forsake yourself; the self has nowhere else to go. Wisdom is an environment; don't ignore it; nature and all creatures offer it freely. If you want to know, then learn to grow, or your life's garden will wither and go. Time is a constant and we are not. In this life, one can only be lonely if they wish to be.

Why do so many humans create their own misery? These human types who act so and think so are the singular creators of such anguish. Sure, perhaps such people or places can tempt such thoughts, but the tempted can still grasp onto an ability and responsibility to not be persuaded into a surrender.

Strange is labelled as out of the norm, but when the norm is strange, then some tables will be wobbled, and drinks will be spilled, all too regularly.

<u>On Daybreak Meaning</u> 04/20/2025 06:09 AM

The most beautiful time of a day is when birds begin their songs just before the crack of dawn.

<u>On Little Steps</u> 04/21/2025 04:07 PM

On must free the mind before they can free themself.

<u>On Politics Hijinks</u> 04/21/2025 07:40 PM

It's plain as the day is long. The U.S.A. Democrat Party favors communism over capitalism. Communism is the death knell of every citizen's life.

<u>On Nose Blowing</u> 04/22/2025 12:22 AM

Honking the horn. Clearing the external nasal valves. Shooting the snot. Booger blowouts. Snuffing and puffing. Cumming. Emptying the snot box. Farming the blow. Hot snarling. Booger sugar. Blowrection. Sticky louis. Komodo dragon. Shooting blanks. Milking the walnut. Bushman's blow. Blowmotion. Vomick. Nasal blasting. Tumble weeds. Biffins bridge. Market street torpedo. Dirty Gonzalez. Columbian flue. Chinese slingshot. Discount double check. Nebraska slurpee. Cake farting. Coldemort. Nose mining. Stretching the Michael. Omaha snow globe. Polish nose dive. The huff and puff. Ghetto tumble weed. Trickfart. Storm the rusty castle.

Snotty Scotsman. Thunder mist. French eskimo kiss. Missouri wind tunnel. Bavarian snorkeler. Cumsnot. Trumping the fakemedia.

See also, Reference: urbanthesaurus.org

On Bloviation Oblivion 04/22/2025 04:38 PM

The Democrat Party has lied themselves into oblivion. An oblivion universe they richly earned at the citizens' expense.

On Righteous Perseverance 04/22/2025 04:57 PM

The ugliest days often arrive before the most beautiful days make a heroic appearance. Some patience and resilience are required along the journey path.

On Human Traits 04/23/2025 03:38 PM

The seasonal changes are somewhat predictable around the world, but only if the affectation of averages are scalable. The averages only serve as a fiction to comfort the human brain. Comfort, too, is a fiction. It is rightly sought, can even be bought, but primarily for the body, as no emotion can be lassoed and pulled down into submission permanently. And that circumstance of life we play upon our minds, as solace, in the uncertainty vines of existence.

On Time Vertigoes 04/23/2025 03:53 AM

Greatest good, greatest bad, greatest indifference, greatest sad. Life's clock, resetting.

On Chasing the Rabbit 04/23/2025 03:56 AM

A rabbit chase paced avoids falling flat faced.

On Two Humanity Levels 04/23/2025 04:09 AM

The basic social structure of every civilization is as follows. The elite class and everyone else. Each class is a bit ignorant of the other, whether by reason, truth, or intentional manipulation. But one social tenet is written in stone.

The elites can afford not to care about the lives of anyone but themselves. Everyone else must beware of imposed elitist abuse and persecution. Everyone else must serve the gods or lose everything.

Is such thinking a mirage? Yes, but only in which desert live the occupants.

Sandstorms further shade the stings of existence. A human cannot see their own back without a mirror, and a mirror doesn't speak like an invisible wind. All see what they want to see, even if drowning in a wasteland sea.

The mind, too, can deceive, tricking us into viewing only what we want to perceive. How we need to believe.

We all bear the mirror face in this blazing, dazzling, deceitful place. It is the only space available for the human race. Make the best of it at a measured pace.

On Measures Equal 04/23/2025 04:23 AM

A measure of caution is equal to two measures of protection.

On Cycles Circles 04/23/2025 04:26 AM

Memories of autumn lead to winter. Memories of winter lead to spring. Memories of spring lead to summer. Memories of summer lead to autumn.

On Commonality Myths 04/23/2025 04:46 AM

The common person is a myth. We are all uncommon in the grand scheme of creature existence.

On Bug Wars 04/23/2025 02:51 PM

I recently had a night dream where centipedes were tracking down and eating ground ants. Have to do some bug research.

On What Biden Did To Us 04/23/2025 03:12 PM

President 47 Trump said it would take 200 years to prosecute and adjudicate the legality of President Biden's illegal immigrant entry scheme. Think about it for one second. 200 years. I'd say that's a literal war Biden instituted against the U.S. citizens. More entries in 4 years than in any other 4 year period in U.S. history. Abominable.

On Reality Bends 04/23/2025 03:48 PM Stay the corpse or play the corpse. Either option is a trick of reality.

On Down on the Farm 04/23/2025 10:21 PM

Little Jimmy cracked corn on a windy day. Little Jimmy cracked corn on a windy day. Little Jimmy cracked corn on a windy day. Then daddy said, "Boy, comb your hair".

On Word Play 04/24/2025 05:04 AM

Saying "I'm certain" is a fuzzy way of meaning "I've no idea".

On Reality Runs Wild 04/24/2025 05:30 AM

There should be a leash law applicable to walking the reality in public.

On Circumstances Puzzles 04/24/2025 05:40 AM

"Too many times" can be a compliment or an insult depending on the circumstances.

On Distance Completions 04/24/2025 05:44 AM

According to MapQuest, a 9 minute drive equals a 90 minute walk. Either way, a good engine is required to complete the journey.

On Grueling Repetitions 04/24/2025 05:47 AM

Calluses of body compliment calluses of mind.

On Product Assurances 04/24/2025 06:08 AM

Oddity is a commodity of no warrantee assurancey.

On the COP Party 04/24/2025 07:03 AM

Basically, there are 3 action principles of the modern day U.S.A. Democrat Party: crime is good; offensive language is awesome sauce; propaganda lies are truth. In short, COP party rules.

On "The View" View 04/24/2025 03:36 PM

When Democrat House Rep Nancy Pelosi said "we need more grape pickers", while referring to illegal immigration, if you read between the lines, it's obvious she meant "our party needs more vote cheaters". "The View" is playing themselves as the fools.

On Socializing Sparks 04/24/2025 04:01 PM

Many times, when we converse with other humans, we may think we are as smart as the other humans, or we are each dumb asses. Still, there is some comfort to take in a commonality.

<u>On Upbeat Vibes</u> 04/24/2025 04:11 PM

Enjoy life. Don't mourn it.

<u>On Trying Titillations</u> 04/24/2025 04:18 PM

Don't let sexual desires rule your life. It's a curse which must be defeated.

<u>On Politicians Vile</u> 04/24/2025 04:24 PM

Don't let the politicians steal your life's ambitions.

<u>On Commonality Passages</u> 04/24/2025 04:28 PM

Too many times, common ground tends to involve a rotted bridge crossing.

<u>On Political Powers</u> 04/24/2025 05:13 PM

Communism transforms citizens into government owned drones.

<u>On Politics, Humanity</u> 04/25/2025 04:28 PM

Persecution isn't listening. It's a one-way street.

<u>On Philosophy Schooled</u> 04/25/2025 05:36 PM

One can become a fairly good philosopher just by listening to a single asshole relative or teacher.

<u>On Governed Sun Dims</u> 04/25/2025 06:30 PM

The Brits will pursue a government funded program to dim the Sun as part of a climate change defense project. Their government has gone stone cold blind, and that blindness wasn't caused by climate change or the Sun.

<u>On Interpreting Rains</u> 04/26/2025 12:55 AM

At home, in early morning hour, a bit beyond midnight, slow and steady soft tapping sounds tickle along the rooftop and glass windows of silent house exteriors. The origin is certain, to my mind, as tear drops falling through the atmosphere, courtesy of the heavens.

I realize earth's weather gods don't mourn for us, or our families. Sometimes, they tap as warnings, and sometimes they tap as rings of hope, but not frequently enough in such a manner as I'd like or prefer.

Sinners, saints, heroes, fakes can hear the sound taps, and make of them what they will in these airs of uncertain swill.

On Alive Meals 04/26/2025 01:03 AM

Birth comes with pain, and so too, death. Each sandwiches life, peeking out from the meal's boundaries, teasing tasty moments.

On Writing 04/26/2025 01: 09 AM

Creating sentences, cheating out a clause. Stretching, then suddenly a pause, then shredding through thoughts until they become lost. A meaning is meant to arise as boss in this abyss. But too many bosses creates chaos tossed. A funny, painful event the process displays, flays, until the mind realizes it needs a peaceful, spaced upon haze to pass over the mind's valley edge, using a peak's grounded ledge where flatland grasses, too, are displaced. The swirl is a bit squirrely. The result comes not early. The digging continues for a potential growth, a rooted vegetable to sassafras the nostrils of an original idea into potential apparent. Creating sentences, ...

On Coin Flips Human 04/26/2025 01:12 AM

For a human, heads natural, tails unnatural. Such thinking is just one life rationality amongst thousands of creatures and possibilities.

On Faith and Fortune 04/26/2025 02:11 AM

The only invisible hand is fate, and fate is not always awake.

On Proper Hates 04/26/2025 02:33 AM

The two groups of people I abhor the most work at auto dealerships, and any businesses with managers incompetent.

On Seeing 04/26/2025 10:26 AM

Open eyes don't necessarily reflect an open mind.

<u>On Making It</u> 04/27/2025 12:50 AM

No one is stopping a citizen from becoming a taxpayer. If a citizen is not working, they have the right to find some paying job. Stealing from a taxpayer is a moral sin. Make your life. Never allow others to make it for you. Assistance is available. Search for it with the idea your goal is to stop needing it. The kindness of strangers is a myth.

<u>On Existence Theory</u> 04/27/2025 11:32 AM

The civilization who put us "here" is god, and "here" is hell.

<u>On Communications Networks</u> 04/27/2025 11:51 AM Every news communications outlet owned by or run by Democrats has been lying to citizens since their inception.

<u>On Questions Relevant</u> 04/27/2025 12:04 PM

Why would a Judge, Governor, or State official want violent non-citizens released back onto the public streets of the community in this United States of America?

<u>On Math Breeding</u> 04/27/2025 12:22 PM

Calculating mating.

<u>On Social Pukes</u> 04/27/2025 12:27 PM

Socialism is totalitarian friendliness.

<u>On Position Plight</u> 04/27/2025 12:40 PM

Earth is a strange place in the universe, surrounded by apparitions and events deadly.

<u>On Writing</u> 04/27/2025 12:45 PM

Life is an arena of ideas and illusions illustrated by those who wield the pen.

<u>On Weather Clues</u> 04/27/2025 12:51 PM

A frail, loose window screen rattles, tattles clues of weather conditions.

<u>On Out of Synce</u> 04/27/2025 12:53 PM Everything.

<u>On Socializing</u> 04/27/2025 01:00 PM

Don't chase being liked. If you do, then you obviously don't know who you are chasing or the worth of their company.

On Idiot Attention 04/27/2025 01:01 PM

Dear Idiots: Read my book. From: A fellow idiot.

On The Naughty 04/27/2025 01:08 PM

Self-deprecation is public masturbation.

On Idea Creations 04/27/2025 01:09 PM

Sometimes the ideas fly into the mind and start nesting.

On Life's Energy Sources 04/27/2025 01:13 PM

I still remember the late teenage years inspirations of a breezy summer day and have been living them ever since.

On Energy Distributions 04/27/2027 01:17 PM

Ignitions unruly rule many worlds.

On Science Goals 04/27/2025 01:22 PM All sciences missions: search for the methods of finding hard and fast truths, then, never stop molding better methods and more stable truths.

On Thoughtfulness 04/27/2025 01:30 PM

To forgot why you liked something is to forget yourself.

On Meaning 04/27/2025 01:31 PM

There is meaning in everything, even in a speck of dust.

On Sound History 04/27/2025 01:41 PM

Runes riven. Ruins rune. Natural results of nature's tones.

(Listen to the uttered musical notes of Andy Williams "Moon River" sounds.)

On Life's Leaks 04/27/2025 01:55 PM

The house and I have leaky pipes and there's not much either of us can do about it.

On Love Stories 04/27/2025 01:59 PM

If you experience a love like the type Andy Williams sings about in "Love Story", then you are historically blessed. The tree branches outside my window nod agreement.

<u>On Life Lessons</u> 04/27/2025 02:09 PM

Like sex, life is all about the mood.

<u>On Wind Slaps</u> 04/27/2025 02:11 PM

A wind is like a caress and a punch, depending on situation.

<u>On Hammer It Out</u> 04/27/2027 02:13 PM

The downfall of opinion is that it is malleable.

<u>On Knowledge Mining</u> 04/27/2025 02:47 PM

Repetition. It's how to stick knowledge into the brain, because if it isn't stuck in the brain, then it is going to nowhere.

<u>On Letters</u> 04/27/2025 03:12 PM

Dear Catherine: You saved my life. Forever, I will remain indebted.

<u>On Meaning Searches</u> 04/27/2025 03:14 PM

To mine for the meaning of life takes a long time. Good merry luck.

<u>On Writing</u> 04/27/2025 04:00 PM

There's never a last entry in the notepad of a writer. All work stares back unfinished.

<u>On Human Ingenuity</u> 04/27/2025 10:53 PM

Almost every dependable technology advancement has been reincarnated as a war weapon.

<u>On Social Frailties</u> 04/27/2025 11:55 PM

Don't expect life to make sense, especially when so many ill-inclined humans are involved in it.

<u>On Inventive Ideas</u> 04/28/2025 03:51 AM

Many new human ideas have been born after significant nature observations. A natural fire became a furnace. A stone became a bullet. A leaf resting on a water's surface became a boat. Trees became a house. A bird became an airplane. A fire cracker became a space rocket. A grain of sand became a universe. In nature hides a way.

<u>On Learning</u> 04/28/2025 04:08 AM

Learn. There's a high price to pay for existing as a fool. The price isn't as high for learning from experience, purposely seeking knowledge, and pursuing new ways forward in your life.

<u>On Propaganda News</u> 04/28/2025 05:29 AM

CNN has been pissing itself over Trumpian successes. For real.

<u>On the Fed Reserve Chair</u> 04/28/2025 06:26 AM

Powell, Powell, he must go! We don't want no government hoe!

<u>On Fed Reserve Royalty</u> 04/28/2025 01:53 PM

The Federal Reserve used to fund itself. Now, they have been operating in debt since 2022 (Biden administration). Today, they are spending 2.5 billion dollars on refurbishing a Washington, DC building into a "Versailles Palace" styled workplace, paid for by the United States taxpayers. Government corruption writ large, for the umpteenth time! (Source: New York Post)

<u>On 47's First 100 Days</u> 04/29/2025 02:17 AM

On April 26, starkly mad and entrancingly unqualified media and journalists held an "awards" fandango in Washington, DC also known as the "Nerd Prom" (The White House Correspondents Dinner) to hand out participation trophies for their members yesterday. How iconic was the show? Ironic iconic. President 47 Trump didn't attend.

The awards presenters where from the Big 3 national media outlets ABC, NBC, and CBS. The awards went to mostly Democrat Party members. Not a surprise. That's how biased is the media at large and their Trump bashing subsets on the streaming services.

Some of the awards were quite odd, to say the least. For best visual media, former President Biden won for signing a trillion dollar bill into law awarding money to any manner of causes of suspicious usefulness and legitimacy, mostly for Democrat Party politicians and their donor friends. The visual media moment not awarded was President 47 Trump's assignation attempt which happened in Pennsylvania while he was campaigning for President. Remember that moment?

When a rooftop assassin, allowed to climb a nearby building and aim a rifle at Trump's head, then pulled the trigger and ejected a bullet that grazed Trump's right ear. Nearby Secret Service Agents rushed the podium and pulled the 45th President down, then used their own bodies to shield the former President from 2 other shots, one which killed a nearby audience attendee, and another that near fatally struck another attendee.

The photograph which resulted from this incredible moment of U.S. history, showed Trump being lifted up onto his feet, one shoe missing, grasping his hear as blood dripped down the side of his face, after the shooter had been neutralized by local Sheriff's Office snipers. Before the Secret Service could assist him to an ambulance, Trump shouted for them to stop, then raised his arm and shouted, "Fight, Fight, Fight". The crowd erupted in loud roars of approval.

A photograph of this significant moment in U.S. history traveled around the world in many news reports, both in newspapers, and video streams. This moment in U.S. history was not awarded as the best moment at the "Nerd Prom" awards show yesterday. Think of that. And remember it. A perfect example of how corrupt and vile is the major media and their subsets.

And President 47 Donald J. Trump still goes about the business of restoring the United States to a world class status at the borders, in the Treasury Department, and in all other Federal Government matters, including rooting out rampant fraud discovered during DOGE audits in virtually every federal government agency.

On Nature Woes 04/29/2025 04:50 PM

I pretty much have a love hate relationship with the bug world. They love to bug me, and I hate that they bug me.

On Cheaters Communities 04/29/2025 05:32 PM

If there's one thing I've learned in life, it's that cheaters never stop cheating. Who on this earth could love such a mongrel human? Other cheaters, of course.

On Political Self-Mutilation 04/29/2025 09:17 PM

The USA Democrat Party has forged a path of self-destruction. Adios!

On Philosophy Pointers 05/01/2025 02:27 AM

Dependency is slavery, almost without exceptions.

Learn to think for yourself, or suffer demands of the ignorant and foolish.

The End.

Sealed with a kiss. Time for a piss.

PS: No weed was consumed during these episodic moments of human life.

Reviews appreciated.

Books by Mike Gutowski
(Available on Amazon.com
as paperback and e-book):
Cratch
Time for the Dead: Zombies-A Love Story
Ariadne
Misfortunes Of Mister Knack
Seventh Ratica
According To Helen
Miserations
Miserations More
Works in Progress:
Thinker

Weirdasms
Cantaloupe
Ruminations

<u>On Miserations More Still</u>
This novella is a love it or hate it story. Some will love it and some will hate it. Either way, something relevant and important will be learned about this era of the 21st century.
   -- M.E.G.